WHODUNIT ANTIQUES

BOOK 1: SECRETS IN A BOTTLE

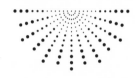

SHELLY WEST

By Shelly West

CHAPTER ONE

"Arooooo!" came a lamenting moan. Abigail Lane cracked open an eye, wondering if an old man was being murdered nearby. Just when she thought it was safe to pretend that she heard nothing, it happened again: "Ohhrooooo!"

Abigail groaned, turning over in hopes of falling back asleep. Faintly, she could hear angelic singing: "Friday night and the lights are—"

Then came another, "Oohhroooooooooo!"

Finally, Abigail sat up to see Thor, her tan Great Dane, howling at the ceiling. On the nightstand, Abigail's phone played a tinny rendition of Dancing Queen.

"What do you have against ABBA, huh?" she demanded, to which Thor simply whimpered. She sighed and stretched over his massive body to reach for her phone.

Thor made no effort to make this stretch any easier, remaining still on his side of the bed. By the time Abigail retrieved her phone, the caller had already hung up.

The first thing Abigail noticed when her screen lit up was the time. "You gotta be kidding me," she mumbled. "5 a.m.?" It quickly crossed her mind that somebody might've died. But then again, the only family she knew was her mother, and it couldn't have been her since she was the one who had called.

Abigail was just about to return the call when a voicemail notification popped up on-screen. She played that instead.

"Abi," the message began. Abigail immediately recognized the deep voice of her mother. "Your grandmother is in the hospital. Would you check up on her and see if she needs anything? I can't go because I... Well, I just can't. She's at the hospital in Wallace Point in Delaware. Ask for a Mrs. Lane. Okay hun, talk to you later. *Beep. If you'd like to replay this message, press—*"

Abigail turned her phone off and stared at Thor. He blinked at her with his big doofy eyes then gave her chin a lick, sensing that something troubled her.

He had more sense than her mother, that was for sure.

A couple of things were wrong with that message: First, Abigail's mother never let her ask questions about her grandparents, so she had just assumed they were gone. Second, she only learned her grandmother was still kicking *after* the woman was in the hospital!

It was just like her mother to drop a bomb like that over

voicemail. Abigail turned her screen back on and forcefully dialed back her mother. Her grip on the poor device was strong enough to strangle a person.

No answer. She tried again, and again, then tried texting, then tried calling one last time, only for her mother's phone to go directly to voicemail. Abigail let out a groan, realizing that her mother was purposely avoiding the conversation.

Abigail had no idea if her grandmother might die any minute, or if the woman was in perfectly fine health, and just had a little mishap. Either way, Abigail wasn't going to risk missing out on a chance to finally meet a member of her family outside of her mother. Maybe then she'd get an answer about her family's past, because it had been a hope-less endeavor getting her mother to open up about it.

Abigail pulled up her phone's map application and looked up Wallace Point, seeing it wasn't too far from Boston. Well, it was seven hours away, but that wasn't far enough to keep her from going. She would go halfway across the globe if it meant finally meeting a relative outside of her mother.

In all her excitement, she nearly forgot she had a job, and that her boss wasn't very generous with vacation time.

Abigail groaned again, causing Thor to tilt his head in concern. She hesitated, but only for a moment. "Screw it," she said, and Thor sat up, sensing adventure on the horizon. "I'll just do as Mother does—leave a voicemail, then become suddenly unreachable."

Abigail called the office, left a message saying she was taking a week vacation due to a family emergency, then hung up before she could ramble and make a fool out of herself. It wasn't like she'd be putting anyone out anyhow, considering much of her job was done on commission.

Abigail then triumphantly looked at Thor. "You ready for an adventure, boy?"

Thor gave a low *woof*, knowing by her tone that he was in for some excitement, though what exactly, he couldn't know.

As Abigail dug through her closet, she wondered what her grandmother would be like. Would her grandmother want to see her? Did her grandmother even know she existed?

Well, Abigail would know soon enough. She just hoped the excitement would be mutual.

CHAPTER TWO

Abigail groaned as she rolled down the window in her VW Beetle. Traffic moved at a dead snail's pace. She should have expected it, considering this highway never went an hour without an accident.

She had made the mistake of listening to her boss's response to her vacation time request moments before. Naturally, he wasn't pleased. But who did he think he was, anyway? She hadn't taken so much as a sick day off in years —not to mention the grandmother she never knew was in the hospital! Abigail had already decided anyhow. He'd have to come down to Wallace Point and drag her back if he wouldn't give her the time off.

Abigail worked for a big-time insurance company as a claims investigator. Though it paid well, she couldn't help but feel like the bad guy sometimes. She tried not to be. She would often go easy on customers who seemed like they were on hard times. Sure, that meant she got less commission and a poor performance report, but so what? She did try to make up for it when she knew she had a scammer on her hands, making sure they didn't get away with a single penny.

In that way, she felt like she was dishing out a bit of justice. She had a sixth sense when it came to those trying to abuse the system. She ought to have, considering her mother was a real piece of work and had abused many systems during Abigail's childhood.

Would Mrs. Lane be the same way? Did Mother learn it from her? Abigail tried her best not to let such thoughts cross her mind. She hoped that she was related to *somebody* she could be proud of.

Abigail felt Thor's eyes on her. She looked down at her lap to see him looking up impatiently. He couldn't have been comfy, crammed into this tiny car. "Sorry, boy," she said, scratching behind Thor's floppy ears with one hand, her other hand on the steering wheel.

She had tried to get Thor to lay in the backseat earlier but had failed spectacularly. Instead, Thor insisted on sprawling on the passenger seat, his butt hanging over the cushion edge, his right leg touching the floor, and his head on her lap. Not the safest position for him, but there wasn't an easy way to cram a Great Dane inside an old Volkswagen. To make up for it, she drove as carefully as possible.

It might not have been the most practical idea to bring Thor with her on this mystery trip. Abigail could've booked him into a kennel, but the truth was, Thor had been her best and most loyal friend ever since she rescued him from the pound a few years ago. She couldn't imagine taking this journey without him.

Abigail had always wondered if there was more to her family history. It wasn't common for someone to cut off their entire family and past, was it? And yet that was what her mother had done—for the most part.

All her mother had from the past was a box full of childhood pictures. She had kept it hidden in the basement. Curious little kid that Abigail was, she had stumbled across that box, and would periodically return to it in hopes of finding a hint about her mother's past, or to uncover who her father was. The latter was a pointless endeavor, but she did at least find some answers about her mother's childhood. The pictures she had found depicted a happy family, a nice small town, something that was worth holding onto.

Abigail had always wondered why her mother chose to abandon such a cozy life, but alas, her mother never told her anything about what had happened.

Maybe Mrs. Lane could fill Abigail in… Abigail shook her head at herself. *Mrs. Lane.* That sounded so formal. Abigail decided right then to stop thinking of her grandmother as 'Mrs. Lane.'

She was going to be 'Grandma.' Yeah, she liked the sound of that.

CHAPTER THREE

The sun started setting when Abigail passed the 'Entering Wallace Point' sign. All the traffic and pit stops she had made added up to a few extra hours, and now she could hardly get a good look at the town.

Abigail quickly checked into the cheap motel she had booked that morning, then dropped off Thor in the room after having walked him. She filled his bowls and patted him on the head. "Sorry, boy. You be good now," she said before heading straight for the hospital, not even bothering to unpack her car.

It wasn't long before she walked up to the reception desk and informed the nurse, "I'm here to see Grandma—I mean, Mrs. Lane."

The plump nurse gave Abigail an odd, almost judgmental look. "Granddaughter?"

"Yes. Abigail Lane."

"I have Sarah Lane as Mrs. Lane's emergency contact."

"Yeah, that's my mom. Can I give you my number as a secondary emergency contact? My mother... She can't be counted on."

The nurse sighed and handed Abigail a form. "Fill this out, then."

Abigail wrote in her contact information and handed it back to the nurse. "So... Can I see Grandma?"

"Yes. You'll find her in room 105," the nurse said, eyeing her.

Abigail eyed her back before heading off down the hall. Perhaps such looks were normal for unfamiliar faces. This was a small town, after all. Everyone was probably all up in everyone else's business, so Abigail figured she'd be on the receiving end of many odd looks until everyone got used to the fact that Mrs. Lane had a granddaughter.

The closer Abigail got to the room, the harder her heart pounded. Was it nerves? No, that wasn't quite it. Excitement? Maybe.

She stopped at the door to room 105 and took in a deep breath. This was it.

Abigail opened the door.

There in the bed rested an elderly woman. Her soft and beautiful features were surrounded by silver hair that delicately flowed down to her shoulders.

Abigail had been so mesmerized by the sleeping woman

that she hadn't noticed she wasn't alone. That was, until a chirpy voice said, "Hi!"

Abigail jumped and backed up against the wall, seeing a perky young woman standing in the corner. Was this yet another long-lost relative?

"Sally Kent," continued the bright-eyed stranger as she crossed the room and thrust her hand forward. Her blonde ponytail swayed back and forth, as bouncy as its owner. "You must be Abigail. Your mother told me you were coming."

Abigail paused, then awkwardly shook the woman's hand. "Are we related...?"

Sally's big blue eyes fluttered. Now that Abigail thought about it, it was a dumb question. Sally's height and hair color didn't seem like something that would run in the family. "Related? Not to my knowledge," Sally said, sounding amused. "I guess you could say I'm a business associate of Granny's. Though I've known her since I was a little girl, so that's why I've been keeping an eye on her."

Abigail felt just a tad bit jealous. Then it struck her how odd Sally's loud tone was. Wasn't Grandma trying to rest?

"So what happened to her? Is she going to be okay?"

Sally's face froze. "Wait, nobody told you? Someone bonked her on the noggin, knocked her right out. Can you believe it?"

Abigail couldn't find any words as her mouth hung agape. She thought maybe Grandma slipped and fell, but a violent assault? "Are you sure? Why would someone hurt a harmless old lady?"

Sally tilted her head at Abigail's choice of words. "I don't know if I'd call her harmless, but yeah, I have no idea. Whoever it was, they fled the scene, and left the door wide open on their way out. Sheriff Wilson caught little Missy roaming the streets, so he knew something was up. Sure enough, he found Granny knocked out cold right in the middle of her store."

Abigail paused a moment to take in all these details. "Okay... Who's Missy?"

"Granny's Shih Tzu."

For some reason, it bothered Abigail to hear someone call Mrs. Lane 'Granny' with such familiarity. Some envious part of her wanted 'Granny' to be hers, and hers alone. She mentally pushed that aside and said, "So what, is she in a coma?"

"A medically-induced one, yes."

"How long are the doctors keeping her out?"

Sally shrugged. "No clue. They didn't want to tell me too many details since I'm not part of her family. But she's a tough cookie, so I doubt she'll be laid up for long."

Speaking of relations, Abigail decided to ask, "So, where's Grandpa?"

Sally stuttered. "Uh, y-your grandpa? Well, he passed a while ago. Had nobody told you?"

Abigail looked away, feeling her eyes start to water. "No. My mother didn't tell me much. She'd never let me ask about family."

"Yeesh. That sucks."

"When did he die?"

Sally thought about it. "Maybe thirty years ago. It was before my time, and yours too, I'm thinking." She then changed the subject. "Where are you staying, Miss Abigail?"

Abigail rattled off the name of the shady motel she had booked, and Sally inhaled sharply. "Oh, there's no way you're staying in that roach motel for the night!"

"Oh...?"

"How about this: I have a key to Granny's place, and I also have her dog. Let me get you situated with the both of them. It'll be perfect!"

"Are you sure she'd be okay with that? She's never met me—"

"Don't be ridiculous! Granny adores you. I've seen the pictures of you on her walls."

Abigail wondered if she had an unknown twin sister or something, because she didn't remember ever sending pictures to anyone. Either her mother sent Grandma pictures of her, or Grandma had been secretly stalking her.

Before Abigail could ponder it further, Sally continued, "And besides, as much as I love Missy, my cats are terrorizing the poor thing. It'd be good for her to be back home."

"Okay," Abigail said, seeing that Sally wasn't going to take 'no' for an answer. Not that she didn't want to see Grandma's house, but she still felt like she was intruding to some degree. "I guess I'll head back to the motel and check out early."

"Great, let me go grab Missy, and we'll meet at the store. You know where it is?"

When Abigail shook her head, Sally gave her brief directions and said, "See you there."

"Okay. I'm just going to take a few minutes to be with Grandma, then I'll head out."

Sally said, "Of course," and left.

The room fell silent except for the beeping of the heart monitor. Abigail took a seat next to Grandma's side and stared, studying every contour of the woman's face. Grandma was a classic beauty, with rosy round cheeks, a button nose, and a full chin. The wrinkles around her eyes and mouth suggested a tendency to smile. Abigail hesitated, then touched Grandma's hand, finding it to be soft and warm. Her fingers showed signs of arthritis, but she still managed to have perfect nails.

"I hope you wake up soon, Grandma," Abigail said, leaning in to kiss her soft cheek before finally standing up to leave.

CHAPTER FOUR

E verything had happened so suddenly that the reality of the situation only hit Abigail once she pulled into the parking lot of Grandma's house. A small sign in the parking lot stated: Antique Store Parking. Here Abigail was, volunteering to watch over Grandma's dog, and apparently her store too.

Abigail had no idea that Grandma owned a business, yet the directions she followed led her to an old three-story Victorian house. The first floor seemed to be the antique store, with the residence being on the second and third floors.

Abigail hoped she wouldn't have to run the place while Grandma was out. She didn't know where she'd even begin with that.

She stepped out, called Thor to her side, then craned her

head as the old house dwarfed her. Headlights shined behind her, and she glanced back to see Sally pulling up. Despite the late hour, Sally was as chirpy as ever, hopping out of her truck and waving. "Good, you found the place." Her eyes lit up upon seeing Thor. "Oh, who's this big guy?" She kneeled and extended a hand out to him, which he greeted with a wet nose.

"That's Thor," Abigail said, relieved to put off entering the house.

"I hope he gets along with other doggies."

"He's well-behaved. Doesn't pull on the leash when he sees other dogs or anything. Shouldn't be a problem."

"Good." Sally straightened back up and faced the house. "Well, how do you like the place? A bit spooky, huh?"

Abigail looked up at the house and shrugged, finding a certain charm to its exterior. Even from the outside, one suspected that there must've been a lot of cubby-holes and mysterious closets within. "I think it's kinda quaint."

"Ah, from your accent, I'm guessing you're a big city girl. I can see how it'd look quaint to you."

Abigail peered at the front bay window, noticing some words etched into it. "'Whodunit Antiques—Solving the Mysteries of the Past.' Huh, kind of an interesting name and slogan. What does it mean?"

"Oh, people come from all over with antiques they inherited, found in the attic, or what have you. And Granny—well, she helps them research the origin of the antique. That is, if she doesn't know its story already. Your grandmother has quite the encyclopedic memory."

Abigail didn't mean to be a cynic, but she had to wonder aloud, "What's the point when you can just Google stuff nowadays?"

Sally gave her a knowing look. "Maybe you can 'just Google it' if it's about comic books or baseball cards, but some stuff has been lost to the past. Granny can give Google a run for its money when it comes to the more obscure and local antiques, trust me. She's helped me identify a few books that I couldn't find much information on." Sally then added, "I collect antique books, you see."

Abigail nodded thoughtfully. "Ah."

Sally shoved her hand into her pocket and retrieved an old key. "Let's enter, shall we?" Abigail and Thor followed her up the steps of the wooden porch and watched as Sally unlocked the door.

Sally hesitated for a moment, peering through the door's windows as if there might be a burglar around the corner. She then opened the door slowly, the hinges creaking in the otherwise silent night. Right about now, Abigail was thankful to have such a big dog by her side.

Sally stuck her hand in and flipped on the lights. Abigail followed behind Sally, taking in a deep breath. The house had an odd combination of scents, a mixture of musty old fabric and the perfume of flowers.

Thor decided to take charge, heading straight in and investigating the store. Abigail and Sally both watched as he dutifully cleared each room, his claws clacking on the wood floors as he disappeared into the back rooms. After a minute, he returned to them and gave a satisfied sneeze.

Sally laughed. "Guess it's all clear then! You won't have to worry about intruders with this guy patrolling the house, that's for sure." Sally then gasped, making Abigail jump. "Oh, I'm such a scatterbrain. I nearly forgot poor Missy. Be right back." She handed the key over to Abigail and hurried off.

Abigail barely had a chance to catch her breath when Sally reappeared with a dog crate. "Here she is, little Missy!" She set the crate down and unlatched the door, letting a frantic cream and gold Shih Tzu out. The little dog looked like she might explode from all her nervous energy, and that was *before* she noticed Thor. When Missy laid her big doe eyes on him, she yipped in surprise then ran off into a back room.

"Wow," was the only word Abigail could muster. She wasn't a fan of yippy dogs. She hoped Missy wasn't always like that.

Sally let out a sigh, said, "Well, guess I'll let you settle in. The downstairs, as you can see, is mostly the store, but there's a kitchen in the back. There are two rooms upstairs. One's Grandma's room and the other is a guest room where you can sleep. There's also a spiral staircase up to the attic, but I don't recommend going up there all by yourself. It's pretty spooky. Oh, and..." She pulled out a business card and handed it to Abigail. "Here's my number, in case you need directions or have any questions—any questions at all!

Granny should be up and running soon, but until then, feel free to call me for any reason."

Abigail pocketed the card. "Thank you. Will do."

Sally picked up the crate, left, and the house fell silent once more. Boy, was everyone around here as friendly and energetic as Sally? Abigail was lucky if she got so much as a friendly glance back in the city, with everyone being so busy with their own lives.

But then again, perhaps this town wasn't so friendly deep down. Abigail rarely heard about old ladies getting bonked over the head back in Boston. What could ever possess a person to do that, anyway?

Abigail certainly wasn't about to let it go. Whoever assaulted Grandma was still out there, and who knew how reliable the police were in such a Podunk town? Come daylight, Abigail planned on doing a bit of investigating herself.

Abigail returned to her car to get her suitcase and backpack, then brought them inside as she carefully locked the front door. She took a moment to forage for Thor's food and bowls, figuring he'd be hungry or at least thirsty. Oddly enough, she wasn't hungry in the slightest, but she wrote it off as nerves.

"Come on, Thor," she said. "Let's find the kitchen."

They walked past the shop area to the back room where she found a roomy kitchen and a small living room. She flipped on a light and found a spot to place Thor's bowls, which she filled before calling him over. Thor lapped up the water as Abigail sat at the table, tired. Then she remembered. "Missy!"

She called out the dog's name as she headed back into the store, finding an empty dog bed on the floor by the stairs. Abigail glanced around the quiet room. "Guess we'll search for Missy in the morning." She figured the dog could borrow from Thor's bowls if she needed to in the meanwhile.

Once Thor had his fill, she whistled for him to follow her as she grabbed her bags and started up the stairs.

Even though she had her massive dog with her, she still hurried up each step as if someone might appear behind her at any moment. Someone *had* attacked Grandma only the night before, so her imagination couldn't help but run wild.

Just as she was halfway up the stairs, an ominous bang echoed from the store, followed by a very loud grandfather clock chiming. *Dong, dong, dong...*

Given the time of night, it was probably going to chime seven more times, but Abigail didn't stick around for the rest. After the first bell chimed, she had bolted to the top of the stairs.

Once she reached the landing, she peeked into the first door in the hallway, finding a large master bedroom with a bathroom beside it. She continued down the hall, finding at the end of it a spiral staircase to the third floor, along with another door to a smaller room facing the street.

"This will do nicely, right, Thor?" Light from the street cast a soft blue hue through the sheer curtained window into the darkened room. She couldn't see much, but it looked homey enough.

Thor snorted, which suggested to her he'd prefer the larger room, but she suspected that was Grandma's.

"Too bad. This is plenty of room for us." She flipped on a small table lamp, illuminating the room. Abigail placed her backpack and small suitcase at the foot of an antique white metal bed. Just seeing its cozy comforter made Abigail want to go straight to sleep.

She closed the door, turned off the light, and pulled the thick flowery comforter back as she kicked off her shoes and climbed in. Thor followed, claiming the foot of the bed so he could watch the door.

Abigail lowered her head onto the thick feather pillow, worried for a few minutes that she might not fall asleep with all this excitement. But, thankfully, her exhaustion was stronger than her excitement, and she soon found herself drifting off.

CHAPTER FIVE

The sound of chirping birds pulled Abigail out of her deep slumber. She thought it was quaint at first—until her phone revealed to her that it was 5 a.m. "What?" she shouted upon seeing the time, startling Thor from his dreams. She plopped back down in the bed and groaned. "Don't you birds know it's the weekend?" Regardless, it was no use cursing the songbirds; she was wide awake now.

Sirens, horns, random yelling—those were all things her brain had learned to tune out after years of living deep in Boston. But cute little chirping birds? She wasn't used to that one bit.

Abigail rubbed her eyes and looked around the room. She had been so tired last night that she barely remembered getting into bed. Last night, this room had seemed like it was made up for guests, though now that she could get a better look, she realized the room was something more.

The decorations were oddly feminine and whimsical, like those of a child's. Abigail wanted to poke around, but at the same time she didn't want to intrude too much. She decided to investigate only what had been left out in the open, so as to not be *too* nosy.

Something on the nightstand caught her eye: an old diary, once again seeming to belong to a child. She decided to open it up, just for a quick look. If it seemed too personal, she'd set it down right back where she found it.

When she opened the first page, Abigail didn't expect to find her mother's name in it.

'Dear Diary,' the messy handwriting began. *'You may not know me yet, but you're about to! The name's Sarah Lane! I'm 10, and I live with my mom and dad in an old old house. I don't have any pets but I sometimes play with the neighbor's cat.*

'I'm a pretty good bug catcher. Today, I caught a grasshopper. I put him in an empty lemonade pitcher with some dirt and leaves. My mom says I can keep him for the night, but I have to let him out in the morning so he can go back to his wife and children.

'I'm sorry to cut this short, Diary, but I have to go to bed early for school tomorrow. Don't worry, though. You'll be hearing from me again soon!'

Abigail stifled a laugh and took out her phone to take a

picture of the entry for posterity. She half wanted to show it to her mother, but she had a feeling the response would be more negative than positive.

Abigail started scanning the diary, looking for any hint of what tore the family apart. She got about halfway with no luck, finding only the musings of a carefree child. Whatever had happened, it must've occurred later in her mother's life.

Worry started to set in as Abigail wondered what exactly had torn the family apart. She hoped whatever caused the separation wasn't Grandma's fault. She decided to stop snooping around, wanting to hear the story in Grandma's own words instead.

Abigail got dressed, Thor staring at her like she was crazy all the while. "Yeah, I know it's early," she said. "But we have a long day ahead of us." Thor plopped his head back down, falling right back to sleep. Abigail wasn't about to head downstairs by herself, so she mumbled, "Want a treat?"

Somehow, Thor found the energy to jump right up and come to her side.

She didn't expect him to call her bluff. "Let's... erm, see if Grandma keeps any treats around for Missy." As she headed down the hall she paused, noticing framed pictures on the wall of people she didn't recognize.

These people could've been long-lost relatives for all she knew. She studied the pictures a little more closely until she found a few photos of herself.

Abigail figured these were the pictures Sally had mentioned. But how did Grandma get a hold of them?

Abigail grabbed one of the frames and turned it around, seeing her mother's handwriting on the back of the photo. 'Abigail, Grade 8' it read.

"Huh..." Abigail hung the picture back up and frowned to herself. So her mother sent Grandma these photos? Abigail had to wonder why, when her mother didn't even acknowledge Grandma's existence to her for all these years. Maybe her mother had some pity for the old woman... Though knowing her mother, it was probably a gesture made out of spite.

Abigail had a sudden urge to call her mother up and demand an explanation, but she knew how useless it was trying to get any truth out of her. Her mother tended to run away from her issues, cutting off people at the drop of a hat to avoid confrontation. Now Abigail would have to make up for her mother's cowardice and uncover what happened.

But not until Grandma woke up, of course.

THE STAIRS CREAKED with each step as Abigail made her way down. Now that she could get a look at the place in the morning light, she had to stop and soak it all in.

The whole house was crammed with antiques. From shelf-to-shelf and wall-to-wall, there didn't seem to be a square inch of the place that didn't have something to look at.

And yet, somehow, it all came together, warmth

emanating from the wooden furniture, the faded paint on the toys, the stained glass of various lamps, and the gold gilt decorations on several antique books.

Abigail then noticed a plethora of hanging plants, all in beautiful shape. "Jeez," she mumbled to herself. "And I can barely keep a cactus alive..." She wondered if she should water them, then realized the plants were the last thing she needed to worry about. It was Missy who could probably use some water right now!

"Missy," Abigail called out in the most coaxing voice she could muster. She heard the jingle of Missy's dog tags, but saw no hint of the dog. "Skittish little thing, aren't you?" Abigail said as she peeked around various corners.

She sighed before noticing two dog bowls on the floor, presumably one for water and one for kibble. Abigail went on the hunt for Missy's food, finding a bag in the nearby dresser. Perhaps the sound of kibble filling the dog's food bowl would bring her out.

As Abigail filled up the bowl, Thor watched from the bottom of the stairs, licking his chops. "No," Abigail tutted him. "You're going to let her eat, mister." She then opened the door to the front porch and motioned that Thor sit outside. She knew he'd stay put—and there was the added bonus of him keeping guard too, as she was a little worried about the granny-bonker who was still on the loose.

When she headed back inside, she found the ever-elusive Missy gobbling up her kibble. The moment the dog spotted Abigail, however, she bolted back into her hiding place.

"Am I that intimidating?" Abigail mumbled. Well, perhaps it had nothing to do with her at all, and had more to do with the giant that was Thor. If that were the case, then Abigail didn't blame the dog. Thor's front leg probably weighed as much as Missy's entire body.

"Come on, Missy," she attempted. "Wanna go outside?"

The prospect of going outside did little to excite the frightful dog. Weird. She hadn't been out since Sally brought her over, so what was her deal?

Abigail headed toward the back of the house, curious what the backyard situation was like. She found the back door, seeing a doggy door just big enough for Missy. "Oh, so she takes care of herself," Abigail surmised, opening the door to see a large fenced-in backyard.

Besides a few benches and bricked-in gardens, she noticed a shed, the door partway open, with a pink golf cart inside. She wondered if that was how Grandma got around, because she could hardly imagine the old woman walking everywhere, and she hadn't seen a car in the parking lot.

She returned inside to see Missy had managed to finish what was left of her breakfast, besides a few kibbles that had fallen on the floor. Abigail bent down to clean up the mess when she noticed something glinting in the sunlight. A closer look revealed some broken glass underneath the cabinet. Odd, since Grandma seemed like a tidy person.

That was when Abigail heard Thor growling at something on the porch.

CHAPTER SIX

Abigail peered out the front door's window, wondering who would be here at such an early hour. Could it be the intruder, wanting to cover up his tracks? She shook her head, telling herself not to be so paranoid.

Outside stood a harmless-looking man about her age, in his later twenties. He was a lanky fellow, one of the taller men she'd ever seen, and he might've been intimidating if he weren't wearing such a flowery shirt.

The man looked surprised as he stood there with his hands up, as if Thor were about to arrest him. Abigail opened the door and stepped out, putting a hand on Thor's head. "Easy, Thor." The Great Dane sat down, but he didn't take his eyes off the stranger for a second.

The man stared at her dumbly, seeming to have trouble

introducing himself. Too tired to care, Abigail said, "Sorry, sir, we're closed. You'll have to come back some other time."

The man finally found his words. "I-I just wanted to check in on Mrs. Lane's place. Water her plants. I wasn't sure if anyone else was going to."

Abigail spotted a house key in his hand, which he quickly tucked into his back pocket. That meant he had easy access to the house, and it seemed like he thought he could barge in at any time... Abigail took a step forward, demanding, "And just who are you?"

He took a step back, aghast at her audacity. After all, she barely stood as high as his chest. "Lee," he said, once he gathered himself. "Lee Lebeau. And who are *you*?"

"Mrs. Lane's granddaughter."

Lee's tone became just as questioning as her own: "I didn't know Mrs. Lane had a granddaughter."

"Yeah, me neither."

An awkward silence fell between them, before Lee questioned further, "Are you staying long?"

"No idea. At the very least I'm staying until she's well again."

"Oh, they expect her to get better? Because I heard she wasn't likely to recover."

Abigail rolled her eyes at the exaggerated gossip. Or was it wishful thinking on his part, because Grandma knew something she shouldn't? "Yes, the doctors say they will bring her out of it soon, when she's stable enough. And hopefully once she does, she can tell us exactly who attacked her." Abigail narrowed her eyes at Lee, looking for any hint of alarm in his expression.

However, he seemed more relieved than anything, his soft eyes unfocused, lost in thought. "I sure hope so. I'd hate for anything bad to happen to her."

Abigail wasn't about to let him off that easily. "How do you know her, Mr. Lebeau?"

"You kidding? Who in this town *doesn't* know her? Her, and her cookies." Lee looked a little disappointed. "I'm not sure what I'm going to do for breakfast anymore. I've been on the 'Granny's Cookies' diet for years now." He gave an awkward laugh, seemingly to lighten the mood.

Abigail maintained her unconvinced glower. "Cookies, huh?"

"Y-yeah, she bakes these delicious chocolate chip cookies every morning and leaves them out on the counter. She can't sell them—you know, 'cause she doesn't have the proper licenses, but she can legally give them away. She's a real stickler for the law, as you probably know…"

Abigail looked away, sweeping her raven hair behind her shoulders as she realized this guy knew her grandmother better than she did.

Lee continued, "People come in for the free cookies then end up buying antiques. Mrs. Lane is tricky like that. Even I'm not immune to her tactics, despite being onto her game. Got a whole bunch of nautical-themed antiques in my house because of her."

Abigail was starting to think *maybe* Lee wasn't the

intruder after all since he seemed to have a fondness for Grandma. Her muscles loosened up a bit, and she even thought about inviting him in to water the plants.

But then Lee pointed at Thor and said, "So that beast of yours... You just let him roam around without a leash? Not scared he'll trample over some old lady?"

Abigail snapped, "What do you think? After what happened to Grandma, of course I'm going to have my guard dog sit out front."

Lee stammered, "N-no, I mean... I'm not trying to start any trouble, just saying there's a leash law here."

Abigail glared at him. Steam would've come out of her ears if it were physically possible. "That's it," she declared. "You're banned. Get off the porch." She pointed to the street, her arm locked tight.

"What? Banned?"

"Yeah. Banned!"

Lee frowned. "From what?"

"From the store!"

He laughed. "You can't ban me—"

"Oh, really? Should I sic Thor on you?"

Lee took several steps back as Thor stood up. Still, he managed to resist. "I'll let Mrs. Lane have the final word on that, whenever she wakes up." He then added haughtily, "Good day," before storming off.

Abigail turned and headed back inside with Thor, slamming the door behind her. Some nerve. Did people around here think they could just waltz into Grandma's house, even when she was laid up in the hospital? And did Lee really think Abigail would buy that he was 'just coming in to water the plants'?

Seemed like a pretty dumb excuse to her, the kind of excuse a guilty person might think up on the fly... Either way, this 'Lee' guy had better watch himself, lest Abigail be forced to show him the true power of Thor.

Her phone rang, and to her embarrassment she let out a startled squeak. Abigail took in a deep breath to compose herself before answering.

It was a nurse on the other line. Grandma was awake!

CHAPTER SEVEN

A bigail hurried through the hospital halls as if Grandma might slip away at any moment. Sure, the nurse said Grandma woke up in good health, but Abigail had her doubts, considering how old Grandma was.

She practically skidded to a stop at the door to Grandma's room. To her disappointment, Grandma seemed to already have a couple of visitors. Sure, it might've been selfish, but Abigail wanted Grandma all to herself, at least for their first meeting.

Then her mind registered that one of Grandma's visitors was a sheriff, as shown by the man's uniform and bushy gray mustache, the same kind of mustache that seemed to adorn every sheriff's upper lip. She noticed his last name stitched on his uniform: Sheriff Wilson. Beside him stood Sally, who seemed to be assisting Grandma in answering the sheriff's questions.

Grandma noticed Abigail at the doorway for a brief moment before Sheriff Wilson commanded her complete attention again. "Come on, Mrs. Lane," he began, his voice gruff. "Do you remember anything? Anything as all?"

Grandma pouted at him. "Mrs. Lane? Why the formality, Willy?" Her voice was soft and shaky.

Sheriff Wilson cleared his throat. "It's a… serious situation, Mrs. Lane. Whoever attacked you is still out there."

Grandma eyed him sideways then answered his question. "Well, I'll have you know that nobody attacked me."

"Then what happened that night?"

"I heard a ruckus and decided to go downstairs to investigate. It was dark, so I tripped and fell."

Both Sally and Sheriff Wilson seemed to unwind upon hearing that. "So this was simply an accident?" Sheriff Wilson clarified.

Grandma nodded gently. "Yes, but it's the darndest thing. Would you believe it—I tripped over a dead body!"

The tension that had disappeared from the room came flooding back tenfold. Sheriff Wilson leaned forward. "What dead body, Mrs. Lane?"

"The one I tripped over, of course."

Sally put a hand on Grandma's shoulder. "Granny… There was no body in the house." She looked over at the sheriff. "Right, Willy?"

Sheriff Wilson became as rigid as a statue. Not noticing a dead body *was* a pretty big oversight for a sheriff…

"Are you sure, Mrs. Lane? I thoroughly checked the entire store and residence after I had the ambulance take you away. Aside from a few items looking out of place, there was certainly no body, no sign of blood, or any evidence of forced entry either. So how could you have possibly tripped over a body?"

Grandma looked like she might've doubted herself, but only for a second. "No, I definitely tripped over a body. A big fellow too. It was dark though, so I only got a glimpse of him as I was falling down. I couldn't tell you who it was."

Sheriff Wilson's frown deepened, and to Abigail's surprise, he took Grandma at her word. "The front door was wide open, so perhaps, if there really was a body, the killer might've removed it from the scene after you tripped over it. You said you heard a ruckus which prompted you to go downstairs, right?"

Grandma corrected herself, "Well, see, I didn't hear it so much as Missy heard it. My hearing isn't quite what it used to be—you know how it is, getting older. But I knew there had to be some commotion going on down there the way Missy was fussing."

Sheriff Wilson looked desperate for a clue, as if he were moments away from shaking Grandma by the shoulders to get one out of her. "So you didn't hear a shuffling, a gunshot, yelling, *anything*?"

Grandma shrugged. "You'd have to ask Missy that, though I doubt you'd get a satisfactory answer out of her."

Sheriff Wilson sighed and looked down at the notes he had taken. "This isn't much to work with." He scratched at his mustache as he thought. "All right, I'll let you rest for now. The moment you're discharged from the hospital, I'll need you to look over the store and tell me if anything seems out of place to you, or if anything was stolen."

"Doubt that'll be the case. I hardly have anything worth stealing. Not after somebody bought up all my rarer items a week ago..."

Sheriff Wilson perked up. "What do you mean?"

"Some out-of-towner came in and wiped me clean of my most valuable items. The ones I had for sale, anyhow."

"You mean you have antiques that aren't for sale?"

"There's a few knickknacks that are near and dear to me. I keep them on display just to show them off. He wanted to purchase those too, naturally, but I wouldn't accept any of his offers."

"Can you recall this man's name?"

Grandma looked up as she pondered it. "He had an odd name. I believe it was Reginald."

"Reginald Grimes?" the sheriff asked, straightening up. "I ask because some folks in town have had interesting encounters with a man by that name."

Grandma mulled over the full name then shrugged again. "I don't recall him volunteering his last name. But he did seem like a 'grimy' fellow, if that helps you."

Sheriff Wilson gave a thoughtful nod and made a note—as did Abigail, only mentally. Even to her, it was obvious who the main suspect was.

This man, if he really was responsible for the body, was clearly dangerous. That, and he had a reason to target Grandma since apparently she had an antique he wanted. And who knew if he got what he was looking for… He very well could come back.

Abigail doubted she'd be comfortable leaving town until this man was caught. She'd have to do some snooping around if that were the case, because she wasn't sure just how many resources the sheriff of a small town could put into such an investigation.

Grandma pointed a shaky delicate finger at Abigail, asking, "Who's that young woman standing in the doorway? She's been standing there a while. I can't quite make her out from here."

Sally and Sheriff Wilson finally noticed Abigail, and Sally was happy to break the news. "Mrs. Lane, that's Abigail, your granddaughter."

Grandma's eyes grew wide. "Abigail?" she asked after a moment. "Is it really you?"

Abigail shifted on her feet, a little uncertain how she should act. "Hi, Grandma. Yeah, it's me. It's nice to finally meet you."

Grandma held out her arms, chuckling at the absurdity of having to say, "It's nice to meet you too, Abigail. Now come give your grandma a much needed hug!"

Sheriff Wilson and Sally took that as their cue to leave, finally giving Abigail some alone time with her long-lost family. Abigail's heart pounded harder than ever before as she made her way over to Grandma's side.

CHAPTER EIGHT

Abigail wrapped her arms gently around her grandmother, unsure just how fragile the woman was. Grandma pulled her in tight, practically squeezing the air out of her. Not such a fragile old woman after all...

Abigail pulled away after a moment and laughed. "Wow, Grandma. You have the strength of a bear."

Grandma looked Abigail over lovingly, memorizing every inch of her. "You're a petite little thing, like me and your mother. Just gorgeous."

"Th-thank you," Abigail said, not used to compliments.

Grandma squeezed Abigail's shoulder. "We'll have to make up for lost time now, won't we?" She winked.

Abigail smiled. "I'd like that." She wanted to ask more about why her mom cut Grandma off from her life, but she decided now wasn't the time. Why ruin a nice moment?

Grandma continued, "Where are you staying, dear?"

"At your store. Sally set me up there, and is having me watch Missy. I hope all of that's okay."

"Of course it is. I know Missy can be a handful though. I sure hope I haven't put you out in any way."

"No, Grandma. Not at all."

"You live in Boston, right? It wasn't any trouble coming all the way down here?"

"It wasn't. I sorta make my own hours anyhow."

"What kind of work do you do?"

"I'm a claims adjuster."

Grandma tilted her head.

Abigail explained further, "You know, I check insurance claims. Make sure no one's trying to pull a scam."

"That must not be a fun job," Grandma commented after thinking about it.

"Yeah. I do feel bad about it sometimes. Of course, not when I'm dealing with a legit scammer. I like to give *them* a what for."

Grandma smirked. "That's my girl. You must be a good judge of character, then."

Abigail shrugged, not sure how to take all the praise. "I-I suppose."

"You need to have good judgment in my line of work too."

Abigail laughed. "I can't imagine antiques attract a bad crowd."

Grandma snickered. "Oh, you'd be surprised. Some

antiques are to die for, as you can see…"

Abigail couldn't believe Grandma could joke about the intrusion that had put her in a coma.

Grandma continued, "I hope this isn't too forward, but I want my store and home to be yours someday."

"Oh—don't talk like that. You're going to live forever," Abigail insisted. She didn't want to think about inheritance of all things.

"Let's be realistic, dear. You're going to outlive me. So this is a great chance for you to get to know the store and how to run it."

Abigail shook her head and insisted, "Let's just focus on getting you back up and running. Okay, Grandma? Besides, I have obligations—my job. I can't give that up."

"Do you enjoy your work?" Grandma asked, her keen eyes demanding the truth.

"Well… No, not really. To be honest, I kinda hate it. But it's a job, and it pays the bills. That makes me luckier than a lot of people these days."

Grandma nodded with patient understanding, letting that admission sit in the air for a moment. "Help me run this store for a bit and see how you like it. Life's too short to be hating every minute of it."

"If you insist," Abigail said, but without too much resistance. She couldn't imagine ever saying no to this woman.

"Good. You can start right away."

Abigail blinked. "Um. When?"

"Why not tomorrow? Time is money."

"But I don't know anything about running a store. Or antiques."

"It's easy. Open at 10, close at 6. Those are the busier hours. Put up a sign if you go out to lunch. Everything is marked. If people pay the asking price, great. If they want to pay less, use your best judgment."

Abigail had a feeling it was a bit more complicated than that. "I wouldn't know where to begin. And what if someone comes in to sell me something? Does that happen?"

"Sometimes. Just do your best."

"But, I…"

Grandma dismissed Abigail with a wave. "You'll do fine." Her lackadaisical manner was such a sharp contrast to the uptight micromanagement Abigail was used to from her job. But maybe that was a good thing? Maybe this line of work wasn't so strict and stressful?

Abigail could get used to that. "All right, Grandma. I'll do my best."

Grandma smiled then adjusted her pillow. "As much as I'd like to keep talking, I can barely keep my eyes open. We'll have to catch up later, once I'm feeling better."

Abigail gently squeezed Grandma's hand. "Okay. I'll hold down the fort. Sleep well."

She hesitated, then kissed Grandma's warm forehead. By then the elderly woman was already asleep.

As Abigail headed out, she couldn't believe how much trust Grandma had in her to let her run the shop. The last thing Abigail wanted was to disappoint Grandma, though she had a feeling Grandma would forgive any mistakes she might make.

Still, she would take the responsibility very seriously. She already knew all the things she'd Google once she got home: Small business 101, antique values, haggling, and customer service.

It was a lot to learn in one day.

CHAPTER NINE

B ack at the antique store, Abigail looked around, trying to get a feel for the inventory. She tried to imagine making a sale, how she'd attempt to get the asking price by talking up the various antiques. Though now that Abigail thought about it, Grandma didn't put any emphasis on making as large a profit as possible, did she? She had been so blasé about it that Abigail had to wonder how the woman made any kind of a profit over the years.

But perhaps Grandma's easygoing attitude was what kept customers coming back. Antiques weren't like insurance—something people were legally compelled to have. Antiques must've had more of an emotional appeal.

"Hm," Abigail hummed to herself as she pulled out her phone to look up a few odd antiques. One was a hand-sewn elephant doll, no tags or anything, perhaps one of a kind.

When Abigail's research failed to provide any information, it started to dawn on her that perhaps what Sally had said earlier was right; not everything could be found online.

Abigail adjusted the elephant's floppy ears, mumbling, "I wonder what your story is?" She saw no price sticker and decided the doll wouldn't be for sale until Grandma could tell her more information about it.

Not that it seemed like Abigail would have to worry about selling anything today. Though she didn't plan on officially opening until tomorrow, so far not a single person had come up to the door to see if the store was open. Perhaps everyone knew about what had happened to Grandma and figured the place was closed. Abigail sure hoped that was the case.

Or maybe it was Thor scaring away customers... Abigail had left him outside to stand guard. She headed to the door and peeked out, seeing Thor dozing off, his floppy lips flapping with every snore. "Some guard dog you are," she said, eliciting no response from the sleeping giant.

She had considered leashing him—not that she cared about what *Lee* thought, but because if there really was a leash law here, she didn't want to start any trouble. Then again, she could easily imagine Thor bringing the whole house down if she tied his leash up to the banister.

She decided it'd be better to have him move his sleeping operation back inside. She opened the door wider. "C'mon boy," she said, snapping her fingers to get his attention.

Thor eyed her lazily then grunted, pushing himself up on

his stilt-like legs before heading inside. He spotted Missy's tiny dog bed, which had been left unoccupied the entire time Abigail had been here, as Missy was too busy hiding. Thor seemed to shrug as he moseyed over and plopped down on the bed, only his rump fitting on the cushion while the rest of his body lay sprawled on the wooden floor.

"That can't be comfortable," Abigail commented, then she noticed Missy in the doorway, staring longingly at the bed. "Oh, do you want to lie down, Missy?" Abigail asked, hoping maybe the dog would finally give her the time of day.

Missy stayed still, glaring daggers at Thor. Thor, of course, was blissfully unaware as he snored on her pink bed.

A knock at the door made all three of them jump. Abigail spun around, seeing what looked to be... a customer?

The spry redheaded man asked, his voice muffled by the door, "Is the store open?"

Abigail nodded eagerly, rushing over to open the door. "Yes, I'm running the place while Grandma's recovering."

The man frowned. "Grandma?"

"You know. The owner of this store."

"Oh," he said, apparently unaware.

By his accent, Abigail was starting to think he wasn't from around here. She situated herself over at the checkout counter, not wanting to hover over the guy and scare off her only customer.

The man browsed quietly, seeming to be looking for something in particular. Abigail wondered if she should ask to help him, or if that'd be too pushy.

Finally he stopped wandering around and asked Abigail directly, "You wouldn't happen to have seen a man who looks a bit like me, have you?"

Abigail lowered the book she had been pretending to read and observed the man more closely. He looked Scottish or Irish maybe, with pale skin and that very red hair. She figured she would have remembered anyone who looked remotely like him. "No. I'm new in town so you might have better luck asking someone else. Who are you looking for in particular?"

The man hesitated, seeming to decide against telling Abigail any further details. "Forget I asked." He looked around, grabbed a glass paperweight and brought it to the counter for purchase.

He seemed to have picked the item at random, but Abigail wasn't about to question her first sale. "Okay," she said, picking up the paper weight, finding a price sticker on the bottom. "That'll be four dollars."

The man pulled out his wallet, handing her a five. "Keep the change."

Abigail awkwardly glanced over at the register, realizing she had no idea how to open it up. "Erm... Thank you for your purchase. Have a nice day." She tucked the money under the register, figuring she'd ask Grandma how to open it later.

The man remained where he stood. "Receipt?"

Abigail froze. "Um, well... I actually don't know how to print up a receipt."

The man sighed. "I need a receipt so I can write this off."

"Write it off? Why?"

"As a business expense. I run an antique store out of New Jersey."

"New Jersey?" Abigail perked up. "That's a little ways away. What brings you here?"

The man waved her off. "Never mind. If you see a man who looks related to me, call this number, okay?" He handed Abigail a business card before taking off.

Abigail stood there and frowned for a few moments, wondering if all customer interactions were going to be as odd as that one. She looked down at the card, seeing that the guy's name and business had been marked off in pen, leaving only his phone number readable.

Abigail looked up the number on her phone's internet browser. It wasn't registered to any business, but it was definitely a New Jersey number, so he hadn't lied about that. But why mark off his own name and business? She examined the card from various angles and lighting, until finally she gave up on trying to read the scratched off information.

She'd have to ask Grandma about him, along with getting the cash register's combination...

Feeling suddenly famished, Abigail headed to the kitchen and foraged for something to eat. After having a light dinner, she cleaned up and turned off the light to the kitchen. With a sigh, she decided it'd be best to close up for the evening.

"Come on, Thor," Abigail said as she started turning off

the lights and locking up. "You don't even fit on that bed, you big doofus."

Thor looked up at her, seeming to register the word 'doofus' as he grunted. She snapped her fingers and he got up, climbing the stairs ahead of her. Abigail paused halfway up the stairs, seeing Missy dart to her bed. After a few frantic circles, the dog plopped down, thus reclaiming her throne.

She sure was frightful for such a proud dog. But then again, Missy was without her owner, which must've been scary for her.

At least Missy would be downstairs to watch the front door. Abigail knew rest wouldn't come easy tonight, after learning there had been a dead body in the house only a few days before, but she'd try her best. Tomorrow was her first day officially running the store, after all.

CHAPTER TEN

A bigail opened up the shop early after she called Grandma at the hospital for the cash register's combination. Sure, it was a Monday, and business would probably be slow, but Abigail wanted to be as prepared as possible for her next customer.

That enthusiasm soon dwindled after an hour of solitude. Not one person had so much as driven by, and it wasn't like the shop was that hidden away. The antique store sat on a side road off the main street, but it was still visible from afar, and had a large sign proclaiming its existence. Abigail had even put out a few larger statues and yard art, hoping that'd make it more obvious that the place was open.

But alas, no luck, and Abigail was left alone with nothing but the sound of her thoughts and ticking clocks.

Finally the bell at the front door jingled, and Abigail

nearly jumped, having been so occupied by her smartphone. She stood, ready to let out her best 'Good morning!' only to see it was Sally Kent.

Abigail was partly disappointed, but also partly relieved, because she really had no idea what she was doing. "Hey, Sally. You caught me on my first official day running the place."

"How about that?" Sally said with a wide smirk as she kneeled to pet Missy. The dog must've known her well, because all shyness seemed to escape Missy as she wagged her tail.

Eventually Sally stood up and looked around. "Sure is quiet around here, huh? There's usually at least a few customers around by this time."

Abigail shrugged. "I only had one customer yesterday. Everyone's probably assuming the place is closed since Grandma's still in the hospital."

"Yeah, that makes sense. The whole town's well aware of her condition. It's all everyone seems to talk about these past couple of days."

"She's a big hit around town, I take it?"

Sally snickered. "Oh, you betcha. And once the town catches wind that her granddaughter is visiting... Oh boy, you're gonna get swarmed!"

Abigail wasn't sure how much she'd like that. "Man, after all these years in the city, I'm used to being just another face in the crowd."

"Well, get ready to lose that anonymity real quick. You're

lucky I'm no gossip, but somebody else will catch on soon enough, then you can kiss your peace and quiet goodbye."

Abigail let out a sigh. "Customer service was never my strong suit. I hope Grandma gets better soon..."

Sally pursed her lips in thought. "How about before that happens, I show you around town? It's not like you're going to be getting any customers today anyway. I still have an hour before I open up."

"Open up?" Abigail asked as she was already grabbing her bag and jacket. It was a bit cramped in there, so she was ready for any excuse to head out.

"I run a coffee shop bookstore. It's called the Book Cafe. I mostly specialize in antique and rare books, which is why Granny and I have a good rapport. We send customers each other's way, since there's a bit of a crossover."

"Now a book cafe I can get behind. It's been a while since I had a cup of coffee. My head's been killing me, but I have no idea where Grandma keeps her coffee maker." Abigail held open the front door, motioning that Sally step out with her.

"She has a French press that I gave her a while back," Sally said as she headed out onto the porch. "It's probably in one of her cupboards. But don't worry, I'll hook you up with a strong cup after I show you around town, if you'd like."

Abigail smiled. "Sally, I think you just might be my new best friend." She turned the 'Closed' sign, locked the door, then followed Sally down the street.

Abigail didn't want to admit it, but part of her was

envious of Sally for knowing Grandma so well. Of course, she knew it wasn't Sally's fault. It was her mother who had cut her off from her entire family. So far, Sally was everything her mother wasn't: kind, accepting, and willing to share.

With that realization, Abigail decided to set aside her negative thoughts and instead focused on the excitement of getting to learn what this town was all about.

She just hoped that it wouldn't be as murderous as first impressions led her to believe...

CHAPTER ELEVEN

A bigail walked alongside Sally, breathing in the salty air, feeling the cool breeze on her face as the ocean air swept in from the shore. "It's so quiet," she remarked. Usually by this time, the city was awash with engines, horns, sirens, and the vague sound of what one could assume was cursing. Stuff like, *'Get a move on, you—'*

Abigail dared not fill in the blanks. "Is it always so serene here?"

Sally nodded. "During the off season, anyway. The tourists sure do make a fuss in the summer and winter. They come in the summer for the seaside scene, and visit in the winter for our Christmas attractions."

It only took them ten minutes to reach downtown by foot, where quaint old buildings lined the main street.

Abigail could even see the water from here, various boat masts stretching to the sky.

"You ever see a candlepin bowling alley before?" Sally asked, stopping next to the first building they came across.

Abigail looked up at the structure, seeing what looked like an old-timey version of a bowling alley. She noticed the lettering on the door, which read 'Madsen Candlepin Lanes.' "Candlepins? Are you supposed to try to knock them over before the wax sticks them to the floor or something?"

Sally snorted. "How about I just show you? Kirby Madsen opens real early. I bet you he's in there fixing a pinball machine right now. Those things always break down on him."

"You sure it's open?"

Sarah got a mischievous look on her face. "Only one way to find out." She tried the handles of double doors, and they clicked open. She headed on in before Abigail could stop her.

Abigail followed. The place was den-like, as one would expect a bowling alley to be, lit with warm lights throughout. A cubby-hole of eight lanes was the main feature of the place, with an arcade and bar opposite it. Abigail expected displays and an electronic score-keeping system, but all she saw were paper and pencils for keeping track.

She then noticed the pins, oddly shaped from what she was used to. They were shaped much like their namesake, tall candles weighted evenly from top to bottom. The balls were much smaller too.

Abigail jerked when Sally announced, "There you are!" She turned to see Sally greet the owner of the place, Kirby.

The guy looked very German with his neatly combed dark hair and the face of a disapproving professor. That was, when he eyed Abigail. When he turned his gaze to Sally, his face softened, though only so much. "Who might your friend be?" he asked with a deep, slightly accented voice.

"Abigail. She's new in town!"

Kirby looked hopefully toward the lanes. "Have you brought her here to play a round?"

Sally paused awkwardly. "Well, no, but maybe later? I'm just showing her around town and introducing her to people."

"Ah," Kirby responded, the hope escaping his face. Abigail guessed he didn't get much business, at least during the off-season.

Something about his face made it hard to have much sympathy for him though. Abigail felt like he'd be giving her an F on an assignment at any moment.

"She is a new resident?" Kirby stated more than inquired, eyeing Abigail pointedly. She couldn't discern his accent, but it was something related to German.

Sally glanced back and waved Abigail over. "Not a resident. She's just visiting. And would you believe it? She's Granny's granddaughter!"

Kirby's face only grew more stern. "What odd timing," he noted.

"Odd how?" Sally responded, almost defensively.

"Odd that she has only come to visit after Mrs. Lane is dying in the hospital."

"Dying? Jeez, you're so dire, Kirby! Granny's on her way to a full recovery."

Kirby paused, seeming to be caught off guard by that. "Ah. Is she now? I am pleased to hear it."

Something about the clipped way he spoke rubbed Abigail the wrong way. They had yet to exchange a direct word with one another, but the peering gaze they shared more than made up for it.

"Um," Sally interjected. "Anyway, we gotta get going. I only have so much time to show her around before I gotta open up shop."

"I'll be seeing you," Kirby said rather sharply, still eyeballing Abigail.

They huddled off, and once they were outside, Abigail whispered to Sally, "Attempted murder suspect number one, am I right?"

Sally snorted again. "Kirby? He'd never! He's just... you know, odd. But harmless."

"That guy looked like he could wrestle a grizzly bear—and win."

Sally waved her off. "You should see his brother then!"

"Brother?" Abigail prodded, feeling like she might be onto something. Whoever was in Grandma's store that night, they carried a body out of the building, so that narrowed potential suspects down to strong individuals.

"Yeah, his brother Dag."

"Kirby and Dag, huh? Weird names."

"They're Scandinavian or something. I think they both have Viking blood in them, by the way they look. Especially Dag..." Sally's voice trailed off dreamily before she cleared her throat and pretended nothing happened. "Across the street's the toy store. Mr. Yamamoto's Toys and Games. They keep shorter hours during the off season, but you can at least look at the window display."

She immediately began crossing the street, paying no heed to traffic—not that there was traffic to pay heed to. Not a revving engine to be heard for miles.

As Abigail followed Sally, she asked, "Is it tough keeping a business open in such a quiet town?"

"Yeah, if you're not smart with your budgeting and savings. Summer and holidays bring a ton of business, so the key to staying open is squirreling away those tourist bucks for the winter, you know?"

"That makes sense." Still, it was a foreign concept to Abigail. The city was busy all year around, and only got busier during the holidays. The only time things ever got quiet there was during a blizzard, and even then, some businesses would still be open.

Once they reached the toy store, Abigail did a double take at the display window. She didn't expect much from afar, but up close the window display housed a slew of intricate automata and wooden devices that looked like they'd come to life with a mere crank of the wheel.

"When you said 'toys,' I thought you meant kid stuff."

"What do you mean?"

Abigail motioned at the display. "This stuff looks so intricate and delicate. Like collectibles to be kept behind glass."

"Oh yeah. Well, Mr. Yamamoto builds most of the toys himself, and collects antique automata too. He likes to explain to his young customers how the mechanics work. Knowing what makes the toys click inspires a certain reverence for them. You'd be surprised how respectfully kids handle the toys."

"I'm an adult and I'm scared to go near them. You know how much of a klutz I am? I'm like a walking tornado."

"Don't worry. He has a store policy: You break it, you fix it!"

They continued walking, passing a rustic Italian bistro, and a bubbly pastry shop, both of which were mercifully closed. Otherwise, Abigail wasn't sure how she'd contain herself. "I made the terrible decision of skipping breakfast," Abigail explained after her growling stomach made Sally stop and gawk.

"I'll be correcting that soon enough. My place is down by the water. A bagel should fill you right up."

Their pace quickened as Abigail daydreamed of breakfast. That was about the only thing on her mind until what she saw next stopped her in her tracks.

"Is... is that a pirate ship?"

They both looked ahead at a magnificent ship, its sails on full display. Abigail had never seen such a giant ship up close before. "It's freaking huge!" she added as she craned her neck just to see the tips of the masts.

"Oh yeah," Sally said, a hint of pride in her voice. "That's the town's famous whaling ship: The Lafayette. And I get a view of it right out my store window."

"How do you get any work done? I'd just gaze at it all day."

"Yeah, I know. It's even worse when Dag's on board, pulling the ropes and swabbing the deck..." Sally let out that dreamy sigh again.

"You are something else," Abigail remarked with a laugh.

"Let's head inside before I make a bigger fool out of myself." Sally then dug into her purse for her store keys.

Abigail turned, having not noticed the Book Cafe until now. The cozy stone building had a logo of a coffee cup set on top of a book. Not quite the treatment Abigail expected for rare books, but she figured she'd understand once she walked inside.

CHAPTER TWELVE

O nce Sally flipped on the lights in the Book Cafe, Abigail stared in awe at her surroundings. The embossed books sparkled in the warm light, and the smell of coffee and vintage paper made Abigail long for a past she had never experienced. She was drawn to a shelf of particularly thick books, and noticed each one seemed to have at least several bookmarks in them, one book even having what looked to be a dozen sticking out.

That was when Sally appeared by Abigail's side, holding up a pack of five bookmarks. "How about Pink Koalas?" She revealed another pack. "I have Yellow Sloths too, if that's more your style."

While the bookmarks were beyond adorable, Abigail wasn't sure the meaning of them. "What's this for?"

"I give each regular customer their own unique set of bookmarks to keep their place. That's sorta the catch of my shop: You can't take the books home, but you can read them while you're partaking in my coffee. The bookmarks are free, as are the books to read. My coffee, well, it's more than worth the price, according to my regulars."

Abigail looked over at the chalkboard menu hanging above the counter, seeing a huge offering of coffee and pastry choices. "Wow," she said.

"Your first cup is free, on the house," Sally offered, then more forcefully presented the two bookmark choices again.

Abigail picked the yellow sloths, then Sally hurried off to get a brew going. "How do you like your coffee? A lot of sugar, of course, but how much cream? An offensive amount, or would you prefer an egregious amount instead?"

Abigail laughed. "I actually take my coffee black."

Silence. Such a long, uncomfortable silence followed.

Sally finally managed to find her voice. "Black. Does that mean... no sugar? No cream, not even a little bit?"

"That's right."

"Is this a city folk thing? Because I can't remember the last time I served a cup of coffee that wasn't mostly cream in volume. I just can't believe what I'm hearing."

Abigail took a seat at the counter. "I'm dead serious. It's the only way my mother would make it. Maybe because she was in the Navy, I don't know. She was also pretty stingy, so maybe she didn't want to pay extra for cream and sugar."

"Yeesh. Okay. I'll break out the French press then." Sally began rummaging through her cupboards, finally finding the odd device and setting it in front of Abigail. "Since you're making me skip the sugar and cream, I gotta make sure this coffee is brewed to perfection. I have a reputation to uphold, you know."

Abigail, a long-time drinker of fast food coffee, didn't quite understand the severity of the situation, but she decided to chalk it up as a cultural difference.

As Sally poured boiling water into the device, the front door opened, ringing a little bell and alerting the both of them to a new customer.

Abigail turned to see a man wearing perhaps the most garish suit she had ever seen. She had to shield her eyes, both from the bright suit *and* the man's incredibly white smile.

"Ah!" he said in greeting. "It's yet another beautiful morning here in Wallace Point!"

Sally laughed. "You're not on TV right now, Dad. Talk normal!" She then motioned at Abigail. "Dad, this is Abigail. Abigail, this is Bobby."

Bobby closed the gap between himself and Abigail, giving her a vigorous handshake. "How do you do? New in town? No matter! I'm sure you've seen me on my hit cable show, The Big Kahuna!"

Abigail took a moment to recover from this guy's apparent inability to turn off his TV personality. "Sorry. Not sure I heard of that show."

The sandy-haired man looked devastated. "Oh. It used to be pretty big." His eyes lit up again. "But maybe you know me from Big Bobby's Big Bingo, airing exclusively for Wallace Point residents at 12 p.m. every Sunday!"

"Uh… I'm new in town, and haven't really had a chance to watch any TV."

Bobby's devastation deepened.

Sally butted in, for her father's sake. "Dad, I think The Big Kahuna was before her time. And she's had her hands full, so I doubt she's had a chance to watch your local show either."

Bobby frowned. "Oh. Well then, what brings you here?"

Abigail explained, "I'm Mrs. Lane's granddaughter."

Bobby's mood improved immediately, and he shot Abigail with two enthusiastic finger guns. "Mrs. Lane's granddaughter! Had I known you were here, I'd have welcomed you sooner."

Sally added, "She just arrived in town Saturday. She's helping run the shop while Granny's in the hospital. Only Sheriff Wilson, Kirby, and I know."

Not to mention a certain *Lee*, but Abigail knew that unfortunate introduction was unknown to Sally.

Bobby slapped his forehead. "And here we all thought Whodunit Antiques was closed for business. I'll have to tell everyone the good news."

Before anyone could interject, Bobby grabbed a bagel from the serving tray, slapped down a five dollar bill, then quickly bid them farewell, mentioning something about spreading the word at the local news station.

"Oh dear," Sally said. "My dad is, err, well-connected, so it's a safe bet that by the afternoon the entire town will know you're here."

Abigail wasn't sure why anyone would care that she was in town. "Okay. It's not like me being here is supposed to be a secret."

"I don't think you understand. This isn't like the city. The whole town's about to come swarming you with attention and curiosity."

Abigail still didn't get it. "What, do they have nothing better to do? I'm just some out-of-towner."

"You're Granny's granddaughter! You might as well be a celebrity." Sally pressed down the coffee grounds in the French press then poured a glass for Abigail. "Drink up, because you're going to need it."

Abigail took a sip, and for the first time, instead of inhaling her coffee, she paused a moment to let its taste sit in her mouth. It was roasted to perfection, with hints of... was it cherry and chocolate? She never knew one could get such a taste from beans alone. "Wow, Sally. If you opened up in the city, you'd make a killing."

"I like the pace here, and the view," Sally said with a wistful smile. "Now seriously, drink up and get back to the shop. It's almost the town gossips' operating hours, and they're gonna be assaulting you in full force!"

Abigail paid no heed to her warning. "Yeah, right. It'll probably be just another day of me dusting things and playing on my phone."

Little did Abigail know a swarm of old biddies were lining up to assault the antique store that very moment.

CHAPTER THIRTEEN

That Monday and Tuesday blurred by for Abigail. She didn't do a whole lot of selling, but she sure met a lot of interesting townsfolk. The first odd encounter arrived in the form of what could only be described as the Granny Gang. A dozen of them came riding into the parking lot in tricked out golf carts, blaring their musical horns.

Abigail dared to peek out the window, seeing the geriatric horde inch their rockers and canes toward the front entrance, each one carrying a baked good or casserole. Abigail held the door open for them as they filed in and one by one set their food offerings on the counter.

Then the interrogations began.

"A *granddaughter?*"

"Why do you only visit now that she's in the hospital?"

"If you're here hoping for an inheritance, you have another thing coming!"

Abigail held her hands up, trying to catch her breath after all the accusations. "Easy, ladies, I didn't know about my grandmother until a few days ago! I'm only here to help her!"

An elderly woman in hair rollers squinted two bespectacled eyes at Abigail. "Good. Forgive us then, if that really is the case. We just like to watch out for each other."

"Is... is Grandma in your gang?"

The old women grew silent. One whispered, "She thinks we're a gang," and they snorted.

The apparent leader played along. "Yes, dear. We're known as the O double Gs, and don't you forget it."

Abigail paused as she tried to work out the initials. "Original gangster grandmas?"

The old women all burst out laughing and took turns patting Abigail's shoulders and pinching her cheeks.

"She's cute," the leader said. "We'll let her live. Enjoy the food, dear. With the casseroles, just heat them up in the oven at 350 for about twenty minutes. And save some for when Florence gets out of the hospital, all right?"

Abigail blinked a few times. "Florence?"

"Your grandmother!"

Abigail frowned. Somehow she had never heard her grandmother's first name until now. Eventually the granny golf cart gang filed back out of the store, speeding away in their carts as quickly as they had arrived.

That didn't make the food stop coming, though. By the time Abigail decided to close up Tuesday night, the checkout counter was cluttered with homemade pies, gift baskets, pastries, and so forth. It had been so festive and welcoming that Abigail had to keep reminding herself it was still a few months before Christmas.

Okay, so maybe small towns were nosy, but the upside of that was the whole community treated each other like family.

The following Wednesday morning, Abigail hovered over the counter full of treats, deciding to make a breakfast out of one of the pastries. She was halfway through her second slice of pumpkin pie when an old-timey phone on the wall rang. She jumped, as did Thor, since neither of them had lived with a landline for quite some time.

Abigail got up and stared at the old hanging phone, discovering an uncomfortable lack of caller ID. "Ugh," she mumbled to herself, worried it might be another resident wanting to fill her in on their life story. It was too early in the morning for such conversations!

"Grandma," she then whispered, realizing she would take the risk for any good news. She answered. "Hello. Erm, you've reached Whodunit Antiques?"

"Miss Abigail Lane?"

"Yes."

"Your grandmother can return home now."

"Oh! I'm coming straight away. Thank you."

Abigail grabbed her things and rushed out, just barely remembering to lock the door behind her.

A NURSE ASSISTED them as Abigail checked Grandma out and wheeled her to the car. She wanted to ask a million questions, but had to wait for the nurse to see them off.

Once Grandma was buckled up in the passenger seat, the nurse finally left them. Abigail took this chance to give Grandma a hug.

"I'm so glad you're doing better," she said once she stood back up, a hand on Grandma's shoulder.

"I think hearing that my granddaughter was in town just about woke me out of that coma. There's so much I want to tell you."

Abigail felt her eyes getting a bit misty, which she wasn't used to. "Okay. Let's get you back home so we can get started with catching each other up."

"That would be lovely."

Abigail shut Grandma's door and headed to her side of the car. She took a deep breath before going in.

The drive commenced in silence for a couple of minutes, until Grandma asked, "How is my little Missy?"

"She seems okay. Is she always so nervous though?"

"Oh, yes. That dog is suspicious of everyone."

"I hope you don't mind, I brought a dog of my own."

"Oh! How do our dogs get along?"

"Well, mine is a Great Dane, Thor. Big guy, so Missy seems a bit intimidated by him."

"A Great Dane! He must be like a bull in a china shop, trying to navigate my little place."

"By some miracle, he's managed not to break anything yet. He mostly likes to hang out on the porch anyhow. If anyone's a bull in a china shop, it'd be me."

It wasn't a long drive, and they soon rolled up into the parking lot. Thankfully, it was early enough that the place wasn't being hounded by curious customers yet.

The moment Grandma got out of the car, a horrific squealing started from inside the store. Abigail drew in a sharp breath. "My Lord. It sounds like Missy's being murdered!"

Grandma chuckled. "It's how she always greets me. She somehow knows when I'm about to arrive home, even if I'm still a couple blocks away."

Soon a terrible moaning joined in with the screaming, and Abigail realized it was Thor. She hurried to the front door, unlocking it to see if he was okay.

She found him hiding in the corner, his paws over his ears as Missy continued to squeal. Now she understood why he was moaning: He wanted the terrible screaming to stop!

Abigail turned and helped Grandma up the steps of the porch, then held the door open so she could be reunited with Missy.

Grandma quickly took a seat on a rocking chair so Missy could hop up onto her lap. The dog then just stared and stared up at Grandma, whimpering sadly. "I'm fine, Missy," Grandma assured the poor creature, petting the fur along her back. "It's going to take more than that to kill me, my dear."

Thor was still hiding in the corner. Once Missy had settled down, Grandma finally noticed him. "Goodness! That *can't* be Thor. He's trembling like a Chihuahua."

Yeah, Abigail kind of agreed. Not a great first impression from her supposedly 'intimidating' guard dog. "I think Missy must've threatened him. Like, 'Paws off Grandma or I'll bite your ankles!'"

"That does sound very much like Missy," Grandma said, rubbing the dog's ponytail ears. "Now Missy," she said, her tone stern and commanding. "You better let me greet this Thor fellow without a fuss. You got it?" Missy seemed to understand, and hopped off Grandma's lap.

Grandma pushed off the chair, her arms a little wobbly, but she was up before Abigail could swoop in to help. She was still quite independent, despite her age.

Once up, she headed over to Thor and extended a hand in greeting. He eyed her, noticed Missy had finally settled down, then stood up. Grandma took a step back, perhaps not having expected him to be nearly as tall as her.

"Goodness!" was all she managed to say before he licked her hand in approval. "I don't think I'll be worrying about another break-in with this giant roaming the halls." She petted him, and he wagged his tail precariously close to some antique glass dolls. Yet somehow, they remained untouched.

"You're a handsome boy, aren't you?" Grandma asked him, and he answered with a low, affirmative ruff. Missy let out a jealous whimper, and Grandma sighed at her. "Come now, there's enough room in here for the two of you. Well, barely, but that's no matter." She winked, then wagged her finger. "So you will be nice to our oversized guest, you got it, young lady?"

Missy groaned and went to pout in her bed.

"Oh," Abigail began, "I should mention... The first day I was here, I was looking for Missy's food, and I saw some glass under this cabinet." She pointed at the massive cabinet chock-full of knickknacks. "I couldn't really figure out what broke, though."

Grandma let out an inquiring *'hmmm'* and walked over to examine the cabinet.

It took her but a second to discover what was out of place. "My ship in a bottle!"

Abigail peered over her grandmother's little shoulder. "Did somebody steal it?"

"No," Grandma continued, then pointed at what was, indeed, a ship in a bottle... minus the bottle. "As if I wouldn't notice!" she said in offense.

"What do you mean?"

"This is one of my prized items—one of the few that's not for sale. It's out for display purposes only. But somebody broke the bottle and returned the ship back to the shelf, right where I had it."

Though Abigail didn't want to start investigating on her

first real day with her grandmother, she also didn't want to ignore a potential clue. "Maybe we should let Sheriff Wilson know, just in case it has any significance. Maybe the killer broke it. Maybe there's fingerprints…?"

Grandma nodded firmly. "Yes. Let's not touch it. Willy needs to see this."

"Willy?"

"Willy Wilson. The sheriff."

"Oh, right." Abigail wasn't sure why she was surprised the two of them were on a first-name basis when that seemed to be the case for the entire town.

Grandma motioned toward the old rotary phone hanging on the wall. "His number is on the notepad right under the phone."

"Why don't you call him?"

Grandma blushed. "Oh, because he'll talk to me forever if I do, and I still have a bit of a headache. He's sweet on me, which makes him ramble."

Abigail nodded. "Okay, I know how that is." She dialed, albeit very, very slowly as the rotary spun. When he answered, he was barely intelligible. "Um, hello, Sheriff? It's Abigail."

He didn't give her much of a chance to elaborate, his voice clipped and urgent. "Would you put Florence on the line, sweetheart?"

Abigail frowned at being called 'sweetheart,' then shot Grandma a look. She mouthed, 'He wants to talk to you.'

Grandma shook her head vigorously, but Abigail insisted.

With a sigh, Grandma relented and took the phone. "What is it, Willy? I've got a bit of a headache, so—"

Her face suddenly grew pale. "Oh. Okay. Well, once you get a moment, I wanted to show you something you might have missed. A broken antique."

After a moment, Grandma stamped her slippered foot and insisted, "Willy, I wouldn't be wasting your time if I didn't believe this could be of some significance. Listen, Ernest gave it to me a few years ago before he died."

Grandma paused for his response, then continued, "Yes, *that* Ernest. Ernest Lebeau. And the man who was bothering me just last week was eyeing it something fierce." After a pause, Grandma said, "That's what I thought. All right, I'll be seeing you."

She hung up the phone, looking a bit miffed. "That man. Even after all these years, he still gives me lip!"

Abigail saw where she got her temper from.

Grandma continued, "He's a bit busy at the moment, but he assured me he'll be here tomorrow at the latest."

"What did he tell you at first? He sounded really rattled when he answered."

"Oh," Grandma said, remembering. "That's right, he was just telling me that he found a dead body."

Abigail about doubled over. "What!"

Grandma shrugged.

"Is this a new dead body, or the one you tripped over?"

Grandma shrugged again.

Abigail wondered if dead bodies were a common occurrence here, the way everyone seemed to blow them off. The city seemed safer than this cozy little town!

"How about some tea?" Grandma offered, as if that'd help.

Now it was Abigail's turn to take an exhausted seat on the rocking chair.

CHAPTER FOURTEEN

According to Grandma, the town was usually a quiet, peaceful place, but Abigail had her doubts. Between the news of Grandma's release from the hospital and the news of a body, everyone seemed to take the day off just so they could partake in the excitement.

One particular theory had gained town-wide popularity by noon: The body Grandma tripped over just *had* to be the same one reported to the sheriff. About a hundred people had visited the antique store, all hoping for Grandma to confirm the theory to be true.

"I have nothing to say on the matter," Grandma would answer, "unless, of course, you want to buy something first." Not that she could confirm the theory either way, but nobody seemed to fault her for that.

Grandma made quite the profit that day, probably

enough to make up for any money she lost while in the hospital. Abigail was starting to understand why the store had been in business for so long: Grandma had a way about her that made people happily part with their money. And Grandma would make sure they bought an antique that fit their interests, so everyone left happy.

Abigail couldn't help but feel a little envious of the residents, though. She wanted nothing more than to insist they close up shop for the day so she could have Grandma all to herself. It seemed inevitable, however, that they wouldn't get peace until everyone in town confirmed with their own eyes that Grandma was still very much alive.

The hours wore on, with Abigail and Grandma answering the same questions over and over, until finally it seemed the entire town had passed through. It was nearing the end of the day, and Abigail was half tempted to close early.

She started to make her way to the door to lock up when she saw a redheaded man pull into the side parking lot. Abigail gasped, remembering him as the first customer she had. "Grandma," she said, her voice a sharp whisper. "I forgot to tell you. When you were in the hospital, some redheaded guy came in here, asking questions. And it looks like he's back!"

Grandma looked up from the till where she was counting money. "Oh? What kind of questions?"

Before Abigail could answer, the man walked through the

door. Grandma squinted at him. He squinted back. Abigail cleared her throat.

Grandma broke the silence. "You look oddly familiar."

The man straightened his collar. "I don't believe we have met."

Abigail said, "But we have. How are you liking that paper weight?"

He blinked at her. "Oh. It does its job."

Abigail pursued further, "Still looking for a fellow redhead?"

The man looked away. "Not any longer."

Grandma walked around the checkout counter, peering more closely at the man. "Is it Reginald you're looking for? Are you two related?"

"I already said I've given up on looking for him. And besides, I'd rather not say much about myself. I know how the rumor mill is in these small towns."

Grandma smiled. "You must be related, then. Reginald had a similar distaste for small towns. But why aren't you looking for him anymore?"

"It doesn't matter. Now, would you be kind enough to tell me what he bought here?"

Grandma frowned. "I'm afraid I can't. I take my customers' privacy very seriously."

"He's my business partner, and he used funds from our business to buy something here. We share a credit card, so I *am* a customer of yours."

Grandma glanced at Abigail, hesitating to say anything.

"You really ought to talk to the cops if you're trying to find him. He's been missing for a while now. I could give you the number to the sheriff…"

The man took a step back. "Never mind. I thought you would be more willing to help a fellow business owner."

He waited to see if that'd change Grandma's tune, and when it didn't, he left in a huff.

Abigail waited until he pulled out of the parking lot, noting his license plate number. She then headed for the checkout counter, finding the card he had given her when they first met.

"What's that?" Grandma asked, watching Abigail's every move.

"A business card he gave me." She wrote down his license plate number on the card, then handed it over to Grandma. "Just has his phone number on it. He inked out any other information."

Grandma studied the card. "How odd. So he's a business partner of Reginald?"

"Maybe even a brother. You seemed to imply Reginald was a fellow redhead."

Grandma nodded. "Yes, they very well could be related. When he first walked in, for a half second I thought he was Reginald. Do you think he might be involved in whatever happened here?"

Abigail shrugged. "Beats me. Though when he first visited, it seemed like he was trying to figure out where Reginald was."

84

"So whatever Reginald had been up to, he must not have told his apparent business partner?"

"Seems that way."

"And now he's snooping around, trying to find answers. If that's the case, I feel for him, but he should be talking to the police if Reginald is missing, not investigating on his own."

"There must be a reason he doesn't want to talk to the cops."

"Yes. It's all very strange." Grandma checked one of the hanging clocks and remarked, "What a day. Let's close the shop."

Abigail turned over the 'Closed' sign and locked up. "Good. I was hoping we could talk. It's been so busy that we really haven't had a chance to catch each other up."

Grandma smiled warmly. "How about some homemade hot cocoa by the fireplace? The perfect catching-up conditions."

Abigail perked up. "That sounds great. I'll start the fire while you get the cocoa."

ABIGAIL WALKED through the kitchen into the cozy little living room that was next to it, while Grandma rummaged through her cabinets.

Abigail knelt by the modest stone fireplace and opened the brass trimmed folding glass doors, followed by the mesh screens. She then poked her head inside, turning up to check the damper, making sure it was wide open. Seeing she was all set, she grabbed a couple of logs from a basket on the floor and carefully arranged them on the metal grate.

When Abigail was satisfied with her stacking, she brushed her hands together and looked for the kindling and matches. She found a cast iron frog resting on the hearth, carrying a box of tall matches on its back. Beside him in a small basket were little bundles of kindling.

She placed the kindling onto some logs, lit a tall match and brought it to the kindling, which quickly lit up, then she sat back as the logs crackled. Within moments a roaring fire warmed the room. Abigail closed the mesh screens, but left the glass folding doors open.

She stood up and turned to see Grandma in the kitchen, stirring a pot of cocoa on the gas stove. "Whatcha think, Grandma?"

Grandma leaned to look at Abigail's handiwork. "You're a regular Girl Scout. Now grab a seat and I'll be along shortly."

"You sure I can't help?"

"Oh no, dear. I'll be right there."

Abigail took a seat in a wing-backed chair facing the fireplace, leaving the padded rocker open for Grandma. Thor found a spot to lay directly in front of the fire as an old clock ticked away from atop the fireplace mantel.

Soon Grandma walked over to her, carrying two mugs, and handed one to Abigail.

Missy shadowed Grandma, waiting for her to sit down so

she could claim her lap. Grandma picked up a soft blanket that was hung over her chair, sat, and patted her lap. Missy wasted no time hopping up. Grandma then placed her mug on a small table positioned between the two chairs, then situated the blanket over her legs.

Abigail sipped from her mug, the rich chocolate and mint flavors taking over her senses. "Wow, this is heavenly."

"I put extra marshmallows and grated dark chocolate in yours," Granny replied before gingerly taking a sip from her own mug. She placed it back down and pet Missy, who was already fast asleep on her lap. "Sweetheart, do me a favor. You see that old chest to the right of the fireplace?"

"Yes."

"Could you open it and bring me the big photo album inside it?"

"Sure thing." Abigail got up and walked over to the antique wooden chest, opening its heavy lid. She found the large album and lifted it out of the chest before bringing it over to Grandma.

Grandma placed it on the left armrest of her chair so it would be close to Abigail, then opened the leather-bound cover. The first page had the surname 'Lane' in gilded letters. Grandma put on her reading glasses.

Abigail leaned in closer to Grandma as she turned the pages and looked at the pictures. "Is that Grandpa?" Abigail asked, seeing a tall man standing beside a young woman who had Grandma's sharp eyes.

Grandma lightly touched his image. "Yes, that's him."

"You and I really look alike, huh?" Abigail asked, not wanting to pursue the drama of the past just yet, it being their first real day together.

Granny smiled. "It would seem you definitely take after me." She reached out and touched Abigail's raven black hair. "You even have the same color hair I used to have... very long ago."

They continued to look through the pages of the album with Grandma pointing out various long-lost relatives and sharing with Abigail little stories about each of them.

After a while, Grandma shut the book and asked Abigail to return it to the chest.

"I wish I could see pictures from your life, Abigail. All I have are the few your mother sent to me."

Abigail remembered the school pictures of herself that she had found in the upstairs hallway. "You know what, Grandma? It just so happens I have a photo album on my phone." She took out her phone and tapped open the photo album application before handing it over to Grandma.

Grandma sat back to reposition her glasses as she looked at the pictures. She brought the phone down after a few swipes and asked, "Is this tiny little fella Thor?"

Abigail laughed. "I know, right? When I first got him, he was half a year old, so not quite a giant yet."

Thor's head lifted and he looked at the both of them as if he understood they were talking about him. He snorted, then turned his head toward the fireplace, perhaps embarrassed by the pictures of his adolescent years.

They both chuckled, drank their cocoa, and continued chatting about their past. After a few minutes, however, Abigail noticed Grandma's eyelids were getting heavy. She didn't want to cut things short, but she also didn't want to keep the delicate old woman from resting. "Grandma, you had such a long day. You want to head upstairs?"

"That sounds like a good idea. If I could, I'd stay up all night catching up with you, but I think this old gal's gotta get some rest."

Abigail shut the fireplace glass doors, then helped Grandma head up the stairs. As plucky as Grandma was, Abigail still couldn't help but worry about her tripping, so she insisted on staying by her side all the way up to the landing.

Grandma accepted her help with grace, and soon they stopped outside the master bedroom door. "Seems we never got around to catching up," Grandma noted. "How about this? I'll close the shop all day tomorrow, that way we can make up for lost time."

Abigail smiled. "I would love that."

"I love *you*, dear."

Abigail hadn't expected to hear such words. "Wow, I... I love you too, Grandma."

Grandma pinched Abigail's cheek then headed into her bedroom, with Missy zipping through the door right behind her.

CHAPTER FIFTEEN

A bigail woke up bright and early only to find Grandma was still sound asleep, recovering from the excitement of yesterday. Abigail herself didn't stand a chance of falling back asleep, so she tiptoed past the bedroom and down the stairs.

A few days ago she had noticed a local newspaper on the counter dated last Thursday, so curiosity led her to the front porch to see if a paper had been delivered this morning too. There certainly was quite a bit of news to report.

She opened the door to find the newspaper on the steps. As she let Thor out into the front yard to do his business, she unfolded the paper and gave it a gander.

The body, of course, was front page news. Quite the contrast to the city's newspaper, where dead bodies were buried below news of yet more corruption.

Large block letters filled the headline identifying the body: Reginald Grimes.

Abigail gasped, though she wasn't sure why she was surprised. He *had* been missing, and before now, nobody had put a name to the body Grandma had tripped on.

Abigail returned inside with Thor and sat down on the creaky rocking chair to read further. She knew the first part of the story, if only because it had circulated through the rumor mill: Some local teens had found the body washed up on shore.

But the following details were new to her. The body had been wrapped up in a garbage bag and weighed down with some rocks. Autopsy reports suggested that Reginald was killed by a bullet wound to the chest.

"Yeesh," Abigail mumbled. "Does the mob operate all the way down here?" She looked over at Thor, who didn't seem convinced this was a mob hit. "Well, you gotta better theory, big guy?"

Thor sneezed and took this opportunity to lay his head down on Missy's bed. Considering his size, it was more of a pillow than a bed, but a comfy pillow nonetheless.

Something on the tip of Abigail's mind nagged at her. The ship in a bottle—well, the ship out of a bottle, as was the case now. It had to have some significance, but what?

Still, if it had really been important, Abigail reasoned it would have been stolen. What was more likely the case was that it had been knocked over during whatever occurred before Grandma had come downstairs to investigate.

But why was there a midnight scuffle in the antique store in the first place?

Abigail groaned. These questions had to be answered before she returned to the city. She couldn't leave Grandma alone when the killer might still have unfinished business to settle. And she only had so much time off before she risked losing her job.

She remembered the man from the previous evening who had been asking for Reginald, and for a moment she considered calling him.

That was, until a knock on the door made her jerk back so hard, she almost tore the newspaper in half. Thor let out a low growl, and Abigail searched around for something sharp. An antique sword glinted in the morning light, as if calling for her to wield it.

And so she did.

Feeling sufficiently armed, she approached the door.

ABIGAIL OPENED the door to find Lee standing on the porch, one to-go coffee cup in each hand. He nearly flung them both over his shoulder when he noticed she was armed.

"Whoa there!" Lee said, taking a step back. "I know we got off on the wrong foot last time, but greeting me with a sword in your hand is a bit excessive!"

Abigail shrugged. "I'm a little paranoid right now, what

with the murder and everything." She eyed the coffee cups suspiciously.

"Anyway," Lee continued awkwardly. "I was hoping we could start anew. I brought you some coffee… Black, just the way you apparently like it."

"How do you know how I take my coffee?" Abigail demanded, though her suspicion didn't stop her from gladly accepting the cup with her free hand.

"Sally said so. Can I come in?"

Abigail took a sip of the coffee, recognizing at once that it had been brewed with Sally's special beans. "Oh, fine. You're unbanned for the time being, but don't test your luck." Abigail moved aside and set the sword on the counter.

Lee walked inside, nearly flinging his coffee cup over his shoulder again, this time because of Thor's menacing glare.

He still was suspect number one in Abigail eyes, so she decided if he hadn't won her over by the time she was finished with her coffee, she'd ban him again. "So what do you want?" she asked.

Lee looked up the stairs. "I was wondering how Mrs. Lane was doing."

"She's good. Resting at the moment."

"I'm glad she's recovering so quickly."

"Are you?" Abigail inquired, peering at him as she took a sip.

Lee loosened the collar of his flowery dress shirt. "Y-yeah? So how long will you be staying here?"

"Not sure. I want to stay long enough to get to know

Grandma a bit, and to be sure she's safe. I won't feel comfortable leaving her alone until the killer is caught."

"Yeah, I understand that."

Abigail was about a third of the way through her cup. Lee was running out of time to prove himself to her. She continued, "What's your deal, anyway? What do you do?"

"I run a ship repair shop down at the marina. I fix everything, from small boats to yachts."

Easy access to the sea, huh? Access to a marina, in the early mornings, a seemingly good spot to dump a body... But then again, everyone in town had access to the sea, didn't they? "You ever do work on that pirate ship?"

"The Lafayette? Oh, no. That's a different beast entirely from modern boats. And it's not a pirate ship; it's a whaling ship. The Fischers used to own it, until they donated it to the town as a historical artifact."

Abigail thought of the model ship, and her suspicions were raised again. "You must have a thing for boats then, huh?"

Lee pondered it. "I love *being* on a boat. Repairing them... Eh, not so much. Boat owners are the worse. Want their boats fixed yesterday, and it's only me and my one employee running the place."

"If you don't like it, then why do it?"

"It was my dad's business. After he died a few years ago, I had to take over."

"No other family member to hand the place off to?"

"Nah. I don't have much of a family, really. Maybe you're familiar with my last name: Lebeau."

"Nope."

Lee blinked. "Oh. Well, we have a checkered past, to put it kindly. Not that I'm involved in it. My father steered far from the family drama. Well, *families*."

"I'm totally lost, dude."

Lee let out a sigh and sipped his coffee for relief. "Yeah. Lucky you, then. Because the rest of the town is well aware of the family rivalry. It's been going on for centuries between the Lebeaus and the Fischers."

"Sounds like a Romeo and Juliet situation. If you don't mind me asking, where's your mother in all this?"

"Gone. Died in childbirth."

Now Abigail realized she might've been too harsh on the guy. No mother figure as a child. Maybe that was why he had taken a liking to Grandma? "I'm so sorry. I kind of understand what that's like. I don't know who my father is, or whether he's alive or not. My mother refuses to tell me."

"I'm sorry for you too then." After a heavy silence fell between them, Lee continued, "Sometimes I wonder what my life would've been like if I had been raised by my mother instead."

"Didn't have a great relationship with your father, I take it?"

"Yeah. He hated me. Maybe he blamed me for my mother's complications. I don't know."

"Hated? That seems a little strong."

"Yeah, maybe. He just didn't understand me. Didn't approve of my interests."

Interests? His affinity for flowery attire, perhaps? "What interests, exactly?"

Lee set his cup down, his eyes lighting up. "Oh, I love plants and flowers. What I'd really like to do someday is open up a big botanical garden. This region is ripe for one, with the perfect climate for all types of plants." He then looked down at his feet. "Of course, the repair shop takes up most of my time, so I can only raise plants as a hobby. That's why Granny lets me take care of the garden out front, and also the houseplants. It's why I have a house key."

Abigail nodded slowly. "That's interesting."

Lee shrugged and changed the subject. "Any idea why someone attacked Mrs. Lane?"

Abigail cocked her head, then realized Lee must've been working off old information if he had thought Grandma had been attacked. "No one attacked her. At least, I don't think. She says she tripped over a body, which I find equally unsettling."

"Wow. A different body from the one that washed up on shore?"

"I'm thinking it's the same one, but who knows?"

"All I know is, whoever did it, I hope they get caught soon."

Abigail finished her coffee, surprised that Lee hadn't done anything to incite a rebanning from the store. "Yeah. Me too."

Lee pushed off the stair rails he was leaning on. "Anyhow, I have boats to repair. Thanks for not feeding me to Thor." He winked.

Abigail smirked. *"Yet."*

They shared a laugh and Lee headed out. Abigail's smile faded, however, when she thought back on their conversation. The Fischer and Lebeau families. A rivalry. Boats.

She recalled Grandma telling Sheriff Wilson something about the Lebeaus over the phone.

Wait a minute...

Grandma had said the ship in a bottle was a gift—from the Lebeaus!

CHAPTER SIXTEEN

I t took every ounce of Abigail's willpower to keep from waking Grandma up. That woman slept in late! After Abigail checked for the fifth time to make sure Grandma was still breathing, she sighed and headed back downstairs.

She found Thor once again in a menacing pose, ready to attack the front door. His gaze pointed to a tall man donning a western hat standing on the front porch.

She let out a sigh of relief. "It's just the sheriff, Thor. Cool it." She opened the door to welcome Sheriff Wilson, who was holding an evidence kit.

"G'morning," he said in greeting, then both of them cocked their heads up at the creaking staircase.

Grandma was finally awake with Missy in her arms as she took the stairs a step at a time. She had her silver hair up in a small bun with a shawl wrapped around her shoulders.

"Well, good morning to you both," she said, and once she reached the landing, she let Missy down. The dog checked out Sheriff Wilson, let out a little growl at Thor, then scurried off to the back of the house, presumably to use the doggy door.

Abigail greeted Grandma. "Good morning. Glad to see you up and about. You had me worried, you were sleeping so soundly."

Grandma checked one of her many antique clocks. "Oh, goodness. I must've been tired."

Sheriff Wilson took off his hat, his eyes twinkling as he regarded Grandma. "I hope you're feeling better, Florence."

Grandma gave him a cheeky look. "You know it'll take a lot more than that to put me in the ground."

"Oh, don't talk that way," Sheriff Wilson chided her, apparently uncomfortable with the subject of death, despite his occupation. "So you told me you found something out of place?"

Grandma nodded. "Right. Yes, this ship in a bottle. It's one of my items I don't have for sale."

"Where's the bottle?"

"In a few hundred pieces, I presume."

Abigail added, "Yeah, I never got around to cleaning the glass I found under the cabinet. I guess that's a good thing, since you might want to check the shards for fingerprints."

Sheriff Wilson nodded and squatted down to look under the cabinet. He put on gloves, opened up the evidence kit and took out a bag, then picked up every piece he could find.

With a grunt, he stood up and towered over the little model, examining it from every angle without touching it. "Maybe it fell in whatever altercation took place that night, then was returned to its original location without the bottle?"

Abigail wasn't sure the bottle's destruction had been so incidental. "But Grandma was saying Reginald—you know, the guy who was shot—had taken an interest in her items that weren't for sale. This ship in a bottle is one of those items, isn't it?"

Grandma furrowed her brows before nodding. "Yes, he was especially interested in the ship in a bottle."

Abigail turned to Sheriff Wilson, hoping to find him just as excited as she was about the connection.

But he simply shrugged. "Why did he return it to its place if he was looking to steal it? And we still haven't confirmed if he was the same intruder as the one Florence tripped over."

He examined the model, carefully picking it up with his gloved hands and placing it in a larger bag he got from the evidence kit. "I'll have the model checked for fingerprints too. Neither of you have touched it, I presume?"

Grandma shook her head. "It had always been in the bottle, ever since Ernest Lebeau gifted it to me."

"Ernest?" Sheriff Wilson asked as he sealed the bag.

"Of course."

"Is this not a model of the Lafayette?"

"Yes."

The sheriff's frown deepened. "Why would a Lebeau have a model of the Fischer family's ship?"

"It's rather scandalous," Grandma began coyly. She waited until the sheriff turned to give her his full attention. "Would you believe it? The original Fischer patriarch, some hundred or so years ago, had secretly made peace with his pirate Lebeau rival. This ship in a bottle was a gift, from world-famous whaler, to world-famous pirate."

"That's quite the tale," Sheriff Wilson said with a disbelieving grunt. "But why would Ernest give it to you, after it had been in the family for so long? Why wouldn't he give it to Lee?"

Grandma laughed as she recalled, "He thought Lee might cave in to pressure from the Fischers and donate the ship in a bottle if given the chance. So Ernest gave it to me on the condition that I didn't let anyone else have it. You see, Piper Fischer had been trying to collect every piece of her family's history for the archives, but Ernest refused to give her the model at any price. It was her great great grandfather's model, after all, so it would have made an invaluable piece for her collection."

"Why would Ernest want to spite her?"

"He still followed the Lebeau family tradition of despising the Fischers, I suppose. He knew if he gave the ship model to me, that I'd honor his request to keep it safe. Or at least I did, until somebody broke in."

Abigail decided to butt in. "Why aren't we suspecting Lee, then? Maybe he feels entitled to the antique."

Grandma and Sheriff Wilson shared a look, then burst out laughing. Sheriff Wilson asked. "Lee? That kid wouldn't step on a dandelion, let alone murder somebody."

Grandma tried to reel in her own laughter, not wanting to hurt Abigail's feelings. "And if some long-lost Lebeau is still hanging on to the family rivalry, I think they'd go after something a little more precious than a ship in a bottle."

Abigail groaned at the both of them. "There's gotta be more to it than that. And think about it. Grandma tripped over a dead body. What just washed up on shore yesterday?"

"A body," Sheriff Wilson hazarded.

"Could be the same guy," Abigail suggested. "That's what everyone around town thinks, anyway."

Sheriff Wilson shrugged. "It's possible. But I didn't find anything the night of the incident, and I combed through this place twice. I suppose we'll have to wait to see what my gal in forensics has to say about this model." He hitched up his pants then gave them a nod. "All righty, let me know if you two discover anything else. I'm pretty swamped, as you can imagine. A dead body is a bit more paperwork than the noise complaints I'm used to writing up."

ONCE ABIGAIL WAS ALONE AGAIN with Grandma, she cocked her head at the diminutive woman. "So you really think the rivalry has nothing to do with anything?"

Grandma smirked. "I do. But old Willy likes to think the

best of people, so I thought it might be better if we investigate that ourselves, don't you?"

It took Abigail a moment to catch on. "Oh, so you don't think my suspicions are silly?"

"Not at all. I simply think two unsuspecting women such as ourselves can go around asking questions without raising any suspicions. Don't you agree?"

"Isn't it the sheriff's job to be questioning people, though?"

"I could tell he had written it off before you even finished explaining the connection. I'd rather someone who isn't so biased look into it. Like you and me."

Abigail laughed in disbelief. "He's not one for solving murders, huh?"

"He tries, bless his heart, but Willy's a softy. He just can't stand the thought of his own citizens murdering each other. Lucky for us, it doesn't happen too often."

"That doesn't really sound like a good sheriff."

Grandma sighed wistfully and looked out the window as Sheriff Wilson's car drove off. "He used to be something back in the day. A great detective. He works a little slower now, though he does usually get the job done. Murder—well, that's not what he's best at."

Abigail had that familiar feeling in the back of her mind —the impulse of a lead. She followed plenty of leads in her profession as an insurance claims adjuster, but this was more exciting. She wouldn't be trying to save some huge company a few bucks; she'd be solving a murder.

"Where do we begin?" she asked.

"Piper Fischer, of course. Not that I suspect her one bit, but she knows every little thing about the Fischer and Lebeau family history. So she might know something about the ship in a bottle."

"Who is Piper, anyway?"

"She's the heiress of the Fischer estate. After her father passed, she started managing the Fischer family's private collection of artifacts."

"What happened to her father?" Abigail asked, all too eager to suspect foul play.

"Died of natural causes. He had her at a pretty old age. Passed away at almost eighty years old. Piper's mother's still kicking, but she's too old to properly watch over the estate nowadays. She's in assisted living now, leaving Piper with the estate."

Abigail nodded. "I see."

Grandma continued, "I know Piper knows something about the ship model, considering she's tried to buy it off me before. She probably won't be too happy when she hears about its fate..."

"I bet. So when do we begin the snooping?"

Grandma looked around. "How about now? I make my own hours."

The two wasted no time in making sure their dogs would be good for the next few hours. They grabbed a couple of sandwiches and drinks for the road, then locked the door on their way out.

CHAPTER SEVENTEEN

Abigail drove while they snacked, following Grandma's questionable directions. It seemed her grandmother was more concerned with showing her around town than embarking on their investigation, considering the multiple circles they kept making.

At least Abigail was getting a lay of the land. This little town had more parks than it knew what to do with. Two separate dog parks, and a cat park too for the heck of it, it seemed.

They passed by a sprawling oak tree, one of its branches hanging over the road, giving just enough clearance for her car.

"I remember when that tree was just a sprout," Grandma said proudly.

"Erm, the sign next to it says it's over three hundred years old, Grandma."

Grandma scoffed. "Revisionist history, I say."

"So are we getting any closer to the Fischer estate?"

"Oh, yes. Nearly there." She turned to Abigail, a big smile lifting her soft cheeks. "We're going on quite the adventure together, aren't we?"

"We sure are."

Grandma pointed suddenly at an unpaved road. "That's the turn!"

Abigail barely managed to make it without flipping the car over. "Jeez, Grandma."

"Sorry, I'm used to traveling these roads in my sluggish golf cart. The government had my license revoked ages ago. Said I was too old to drive. Can you believe it?"

"Sorta."

They headed up the hill, taking a turn around a thick gathering of trees. Then Abigail saw it: the Fischer estate.

She would have believed it was an old plantation given the multiple Antebellum-styled mansions on the property, but then again this was too far up North. "Look at this place!" Abigail said, regarding the massive columns in front of the main house. "What's the family business, again?"

"Whaling. I mean, back when that was a living. Since then they invested and reinvested their fortunes rather prudently in other businesses, and it's paid off big for them."

"Wow." Abigail pulled up around the long circular driveway, seeing several classic cars ranging from the 20s to the 60s. "Somebody in the family a car collector?"

"Those are all cars that have been kept in the family. As fortunate as they are, they believe in keeping things running rather than upgrading to something new every year. That philosophy is why the Lafayette is still afloat, so I certainly respect that."

"Yeah, that's kinda awesome."

They got out of her car, the warm sun making them feel more than welcomed. But were they? "Uh, Grandma?"

"Yes, dear?"

"We *are* allowed to just show up on their estate, right? They wouldn't consider it trespassing?" In Abigail's line of work, she had dealt with her share of disgruntled landowners who thought she was asking one question too many.

Grandma shook her head. "Don't worry, dear. Look how antiquated they live. If they're going to shoot us, they'll have to prime their muskets first. That'll give us plenty of time to scram." She winked.

Abigail watched in disbelief as the kindly old lady took the lead, heading straight for the front door.

Grandma rang the doorbell, and after about a minute, someone finally answered, a young redheaded woman with a perky nose and wide eyes. "Mrs. Lane!" she said, coming in for a hug. She then noticed Abigail. "Who's your friend?"

"My granddaughter, Abigail. She's come down from Boston just to see her old granny."

Piper spread her arms, hugging Abigail whether she liked it or not. "Abigail! You look just like those old pictures of Mrs. Lane! Only not so black and white." She laughed, then motioned they come inside. "What brings you two down here?"

"Not good news, I'm afraid," Grandma said, looking down. "That ship in a bottle that Ernest had gifted me before he died... Well, it's in evidence now down at the police station."

Piper spun around. "Goodness! Why?"

"It appears to have been knocked over in the scuffle that produced the dead body I tripped over."

Piper frowned and asked hesitantly, "Uh, dead body?"

"Oh, you haven't heard? There was a dead body in my home. It seemed that an altercation took place in the middle of the night, in my humble little antique shop. Can you believe it?"

Piper blinked her huge eyes. "The world's gone crazy."

"Indeed. And the body had disappeared not long after I tripped over it, leading people to believe I was seeing things again."

Piper snickered. "Oh yeah, like your friend Mrs. Applebaum?"

"I'll have you know Mrs. Applebaum is very real. And so was this body. He washed up on shore just yesterday, with a bullet wound in his chest."

Piper looked dumbfounded. "That's insane. I don't know how I could have missed all this news. I was binge-watching some old BBC historical dramas at home for a week. You know I'm a sucker for them, but to think even bigger drama was happening just outside my window! Come on, let's find somewhere to sit."

They walked down a grand hall full of giant nautical paintings, their steps echoing on the pristine black and white linoleum floors. They took a turn through a huge doorway into what looked like a museum.

Glass displays lined the walls, full of vintage clothing and nautical memorabilia. Individual lights showcased the items scattered throughout the room. The walls were recessed with shelves lined with antique books from the floor to the high paneled ceiling, with a tall floating ladder resting against one bookshelf.

Silky red drapes were pulled back to reveal long beveled glass windows. Colorful oriental rugs brought out the fall palette of the Victorian-styled furniture that rested on them. The stained glass doors opened to the courtyard below, letting in a cool breeze.

Piper took a seat on an excessively large velvet recliner. "Sit, please. I need a second to process everything." Once everyone was seated, Piper continued, "So did they identify the body?"

Grandma nodded. "An out-of-towner. Reginald Grimes."

Piper's eyes seemed to glow redder than her hair. "Reginald! I *hate* that grimy little—" She stopped herself before she said something uncouth. She then let out a nervous laugh. "Heh, way to incriminate myself, huh? But Netflix will confirm I have indeed been watching nothing but British dramas the past week, so I have an alibi, albeit an embarrassing one."

"You're not under any suspicion," Grandma assured her. "But maybe you could enlighten us regarding why you despise Reginald?"

Piper let out an incredulous laugh at the thought of him. "He comes storming down here, looking to buy up historical artifacts, ones tied heavily to our local history, right? My family's history. You know how I feel about that, so of course I wasn't kind to him. I don't trust some big city boy to treat these antiques with the reverence they deserve. It's not even like he runs a museum or something. *I* do, and he comes here telling me, 'Everybody's got a price,' wanting this and that. I told him to shove it and get off my property before I loaded up my musket!"

Grandma shot Abigail an amused look before turning back to Piper. "So he got nothing off you?"

"No."

"No chance he broke in after?"

"What? I-I don't think so. He'd have to be a master thief to get past this home's security system."

"I ask because it seems he broke into my store. So you have no family member you think he could have talked into selling him a piece instead?"

"You should know. The whole Fischer family is as protective of our estate as a dragon on its mound of gold. It's what's preserved our way of life as long as it has." She paused. "Except..."

Abigail and Grandma leaned forward.

"Well, you know. The Lebeaus inexplicably had a couple of Fischer artifacts in their possession. Letters that my great great grandfather had written his pirate rival long ago. And of course that ship in a bottle. Reginald, that smarmy little... He was flaunting the fact that he had bought those letters off Ernest, and that I'd never get to see them unless I opened up the archives for his perusal."

Grandma asked, "Well, did you?"

"No. I denied his offer, but boy, was it tempting. Who knows what historical information those letters could have provided? Can you imagine how juicy an exchange between a world-famous whaler and a notorious pirate could be?"

Grandma clarified, "If he had the Fischer side of the letter exchange, wouldn't that mean you have the Lebeau side of it?"

Piper nodded. "In fact, I do. But the letters are rather cryptic. I could never understand them, and thought that maybe if I had the full exchange, it'd all make more sense. Seems Reginald thought the same thing. It's a shame Ernest sold them, because I know if Lee had inherited the letters, he'd have been a lot more willing to let me have a look at them. He's not caught up in this silly rivalry."

"Such a pity," Grandma commented.

Abigail grew silent. She wasn't so sure of Lee's innocence. If Lee was the last Lebeau around, maybe that was motive enough to plot something against the Fischers. It all came back to the broken ship bottle and the open front door. Lee had a key to the store…

When Piper turned to wipe a speck of dust off a decorative plate, Abigail glanced at Grandma, who responded to her with a sneaky wink. Without a word exchanged between them, they both seemed to understand that they had gotten more than enough information from this trip.

"Oh dear," Grandma said in an exaggerated elderly voice, catching Piper's attention again. "It's past time for my afternoon nap."

Piper straightened up. "Oh, don't let me keep you! I've been known to ramble on and on when you get me on the right topic." She showed the two of them out, saying in farewell, "Feel free to stop by any time. You know you're welcomed."

Grandma's eyes twinkled at Piper. "Of course. You stay safe now. There's a murderer on the loose."

As they headed down the steps, Abigail laughed in disbelief. "Way to say goodbye to someone, Grandma."

Just before Grandma tucked into the passenger seat, she stated, "I need her alive. She's a great source of information."

Abigail laughed again, not expecting such a gingerly old woman to be so macabre.

She was starting to see where she got it from.

CHAPTER EIGHTEEN

The drive back gave Abigail and Grandma time to digest all the new information. Abigail started, "So Piper really hates Reginald's guts, doesn't she?"

"Yes. I suspect she must be tickled pink to know he's no longer amongst the living."

"You don't think she has a good motive for murder?"

"Piper's a firecracker, but I highly doubt she's a murderer on top of that. Sure, I wouldn't put it past her to kick a man in his nether regions, but she doesn't have the disposition to murder someone."

"I dunno. She has the money. Even if she couldn't stomach it, she could've hired someone."

"If a squabble between two strangers was all it took to drive one to murder, then we'd all be dead. We'll need better evidence than what we have."

"Yeah, I guess you're right." Abigail stopped at a red light and thoughtfully ran her hands around the oversized steering wheel. "Well, you might not want to hear it, but I think we should look into Lee next."

"I'll hear it. What's your theory?"

"Whoever was in your store that night, they didn't force their way in. Lee has a key to the place, doesn't he? That, and his father Ernest had sold some letters to Reginald—letters Lee might have felt entitled to."

"What are you getting at?"

"A motive for Lee to kill the man. And another thing: How did Ernest die? Could Reginald have had something to do with it?"

"Sounds like a bit of a leap. Ernest had a huge drinking problem, and eventually it caught up to him."

"How?"

"He'd often get terribly drunk when he fished, and so one day the inevitable happened. His boat washed up on shore empty, without its captain."

"That's not a nice way to go. But I still think Lee could have it out for Reginald. The letters Ernest sold him could be worth something, considering their history. Lee hates doing boat repair. Maybe he saw those letters as a way out? A way to pursue something else he'd rather be doing? I mean, I keep going back to him having a key to the place. When I was staying at your store by myself, he tried to return early in the morning. Maybe he wanted to tie up loose ends."

Grandma's brows furrowed at she tapped on her lips.

116

Finally she relented. "Oh, all right. Now you've got me curi-ous. But we need to be casual about it. If he's innocent and he realizes I suspected him, I don't think he'd ever forgive me."

"We don't have to ask him directly. I remember him saying he had an employee."

"Oh, right. The young man he works with, Antonio. Good thinking." Grandma's eyes lit up. "And lucky us, Thursday is one of Lee's days off from the repair shop, leaving Antonio to take the reins. Let's first stop by the house. I'll grab some cookies to butter him up."

Abigail smirked. "The game is afoot!"

AFTER RETRIEVING HER COOKIES, Grandma directed Abigail to the marina. As Abigail pulled down the small road, she commented, "Thought this place would be a bit more happening."

Aside from a few small boats in a dry storage warehouse, the entire marina looked long abandoned.

Grandma said, "Just wait until tourist season. Then you can't find a place to park."

Abigail came to a stop in front of the Lebeau Boat Repair shop, seeing only a small truck parked in the lot. "I'm guessing that's Antonio's truck?"

"Must be. I never come down here."

They got out of the car, Grandma carrying a small plate

of her homemade cookies. They made their way to the shop, finding a young tanned man smoking by the water. He had a faraway look, his sleeves rolled up to reveal some nautical tattoos.

The man looked dead tired and none too friendly, but when he heard their approach, his attitude changed. He turned to see Grandma, perking up when he saw she had brought baked goods. "Mrs. Lane," he said in greeting, and he tossed his cigarette into the water. "You do delivery now?"

"Only since my granddaughter came into town," Grandma answered with a wink, handing the plate over to him.

Antonio dug straight into the pile of cookies. "Mm, you gotta tell me the recipe one of these days."

Grandma smiled. "You'll have to strangle it out of me."

Antonio laughed awkwardly, then nodded at Abigail. "So, the granddaughter?"

Abigail held a hand out, knowing full well it'd be difficult for him to shake it with the plate in his grip. Still, he managed to balance it in one hand and return the gesture. "Abigail," she said in introduction.

"Antonio. Nice of you to take my place as the new person in town."

"New, huh?" Abigail asked, her head cocked.

Grandma explained, "We don't get many new residents. Only tourists. So even though he's been here for a good six months now, he's still the new guy in town."

Abigail eyed him. "I see. Well, you still are, since I'm only here temporarily."

"Oh, that so?" Antonio asked as he downed another cookie. "Too bad. Not a lot of new blood around here. At least not during the off-season."

"What brought you here?" Abigail asked, watching his face closely.

Antonio shrugged. "You know. Work."

"You moved all the way down to this quiet old town to fix boats?"

Antonio nodded, having trouble swallowing his cookie. "Yeah, Lee couldn't run the place all by himself ever since his father... you know. So he advertised for help. I used to live an hour away, but when I saw the ad and looked up Wallace Point, the town just called out to me. Guess I was fed up with the big city, you know? So I applied, got the job, and made the move."

Abigail's eyes narrowed as Grandma changed the subject. "So how has business been?"

Antonio used a cookie to point at a medium-sized ship in dry dock. "Working on her right now. The moron who owns it crashed into a bunch of rocks. He thinks yelling at us every couple of hours over the phone will make things go faster, but that just ain't how it works."

"Out of towner?" Grandma inquired.

"Yeah, on his way to Maine. Never planned on getting caught up in this little town. Maybe he shoulda thought about it before sailing drunk. I been working on it almost nonstop, but these things take time, ya know? Ruined my Friday night fixing just half of what's wrong with the boat."

Grandma and Abigail shared a look. Friday was the night of the incident. Abigail asked, "Did Lee ruin his Friday night too?"

"Yup. Well, maybe it wasn't ruined for him, per se. He ain't gotta nightlife like I do. Doubt the owner cares about ruining my weekend either."

Grandma nodded. "Oh, I know the type. You just can't please some customers. I had someone come in not that long ago thinking he could buy something that wasn't for sale. Put up quite the fuss about it too. Imagine my surprise when a few days later his body washed up on shore!"

Both Grandma and Abigail waited for a reaction. Antonio merely blinked at them before lighting up in realization. "Oh, that Reginald guy that was in the newspaper?"

"That's the one."

Antonio paused, looking around as if to make sure they were alone. Seeing there wasn't another soul for miles, he said in a lowered voice, "You know, I was at the bowling alley last week. Not that bowling's my scene, but it's the cheapest place in town for a beer."

Abigail and Grandma listened, waiting for something relevant.

Antonio continued, "And so that Reginald guy was there. He and Kirby got into a rip-roaring argument. Most exciting thing to happen here for a month!"

Grandma leaned in closer. "You don't say?"

"Yeah. Kirby always had a short temper. It's not like it's the first time he kicked a belligerent drunk out of the place, but this was something else. I never saw him upset like that before."

Abigail asked, "Any idea what they were arguing about?"

"I don't know. Neither of 'em were making much sense. Reginald was drunk, and Kirby's got an accent, so it was hard to tell. Something about that old ship, and Reginald questioning why Kirby had donated so much money toward its preservation."

"The Lafayette?" Grandma asked.

"Yeah, that's the one. I guess Reginald thinks Kirby has some ulterior motive. Some big plan for the ship. What he could possibly be planning for some ancient boat's beyond me, though."

"That's odd," Abigail said. She tried to rack her brain for what little she knew about the ship, but she drew a blank.

"You're telling me. Eventually Kirby had enough, got beet red, then physically picked Reginald up and threw him out to the curb. Seems like a dumb thing to get mad about, but I guess Vikings have a temper!"

Abigail briefly recalled what Sally had told her, now that she heard the word 'Viking.' Both Kirby and his brother... Dag, was it? They had Viking roots. Scandinavian. But what significance could the Lafayette have to them? It was a ship from an era long after the Vikings.

Grandma looked at her wrist, seeing the time. "Oh dear! It's past time for my afternoon nap!"

Abigail suppressed a snort. Was that how Grandma got out of every social engagement? Either way, it was an effective tactic, as nobody wanted to keep someone as elderly as Grandma from taking a nap.

"Oh, I'll let you go then," Antonio said, finishing the last cookie and handing Grandma the plate. "It's been nice talking to you. And nice meeting you, Abigail." He smiled at her. "Maybe I'll see you around at the bowling alley?"

"Yeah, sure," Abigail said, having no intention of that happening. She knew his type.

The two of them headed back to the car, Abigail wondering if Kirby really could have something to do with what had transpired. He had seemed like a nice guy when Sally introduced him to her. Quiet and odd, but nice.

Either way, she figured Grandma would have more to say on the topic once they were in the privacy of her car.

CHAPTER NINETEEN

Abigail made her way back to the antique store, starting to get familiar with the main roads now. Grandma looked deep in thought, gazing out the window as she undoubtedly pondered everything Antonio had said.

Abigail decided to start first. "So, Kirby's got some major beef with Reginald. More than anyone else we've talked to, it seems."

"I'm not surprised. A strong, quiet type like Kirby isn't about to humor someone as sordid as Reginald."

"But the fight they had, it sounds like a bit more than just being annoyed at the guy. I wonder if Sheriff Wilson knows about this scuffle?"

"And why should he know?"

Abigail wasn't sure why that was even a question. "He's

the one on the case, isn't he? We should inform him about any potential suspects."

"Kirby's a hard-working man. I wouldn't want to give him any trouble unless we had more on him. Reginald made enemies everywhere he went, so I'm not so sure Kirby is a special case."

"Yeah, but there's the connection with his brother working on the Lafayette, the same ship your broken model's based off... Things are starting to add up a bit."

"To what? Piper is connected to the Lafayette too. And so am I, I suppose. We need more than that."

As they parked back at the antique store, Grandma turned to Abigail and suggested, "You know, Kirby's very close to his younger brother, Dag. Dag's a nice young man—scrappy, but a person of strong character. I don't see him burying any bodies for his brother, as close as they are. Viking though he may be, he hasn't the heart for that sort of business."

"So you think we should talk to Dag?"

"No, I think *you* should talk to him. I'm a bit tired after two interviews."

Though Grandma unbuckled and opened her door, Abigail remained seated. "I don't want to go nosing around by myself. Don't you think we make a good team?"

Missy's hysterical screaming began, followed soon by Thor's moaning. Grandma shook her head and stepped out of the car. "I can't leave Missy by herself for too long."

Abigail groaned.

"And besides," Grandma said, ducking down to peer into the car at a very reluctant Abigail. "A beautiful young woman like yourself, inquiring all about Dag... He'll open up like a well-read book."

Abigail saw she had lost this battle. "If you say so. But I don't have the pretense of a cookie delivery to meet up with him. Where do I even begin?"

"Just pretend you're there for a tour of the ship, then get him talking. I doubt there will be many tourists around on a weekday, so you'll have him and the ship all to yourself. Go. I'll take care of our dogs."

By now, Missy's wailing had reached new heights of ear-piercing. Grandma hurried up the porch stairs, not giving Abigail a chance to say much else. Oh well, Abigail had already interviewed two people today. Why not make it three? She didn't have much time anyhow.

This murder needed to be solved fast, and if it was all up to Abigail, then so be it.

ABIGAIL MADE it to downtown Wallace Point in under two minutes. "I could have probably just walked," she mumbled to herself as she looked for somewhere to park. It was starting to make sense how Grandma managed to get around with only a golf cart, since everything was so close by.

Abigail parked within eyesight of the Lafayette. "Here

goes," she said to herself in an attempt to gather up her courage.

Her stomach growled in protest. She looked at the time. 4 o'clock, and she hadn't eaten anything but a small sandwich.

Her eyes wandered over to Sally's Book Cafe. It was right in view of the Lafayette, which reminded Abigail about Sally's guilty pleasure of watching Dag work.

Abigail knew what she had to do. She'd swing by the Book Cafe for something to eat, then talk Sally into chatting up Dag with her.

Abigail got out of her car and followed the sweet aroma of pastries and coffee. She stepped into the Book Cafe to find Sally putting away coffee appliances.

Before Sally turned to see her guest, she said, "Sorry, closing up for the day." Then she saw who it was. "Abigail! I didn't expect you to come by. It's nice to see you again."

"Likewise. Could I possibly trouble you for a snack before you close? I only had a sandwich today so I'm famished."

"Perfect, I'll fix up something for us both. Coffee? As black as a deep-sea abyss, of course."

"Of course."

Sally pulled out her French press. "Busy day?"

Abigail took a seat at the counter. "Yeah. Let's just say Grandma and I have done a bit of sleuthing."

Sally's eyes grew big and she lowered her voice. "In regards to the murder? Have you found any leads?"

"A few. Nothing concrete yet, but the next place I'm

snooping is right across the street."

Sally pondered for a moment. "The Lafayette?"

"You got it."

"Oh, Dag isn't a suspect, is he?" With a concerned furrow of her brows, Sally looked braced for devastation.

"No, but maybe he knows something."

Sally let out a relieved sigh. "Good. I don't know what I'd do without my eye candy. He's so dreamy, the way he works that ship."

"Why don't you tag along? I'm gonna feel pretty awkward getting a tour of the Lafayette all by myself."

Sally's skin flushed and she turned to tend to the French press. "I couldn't. I'll become a blubbering fool in front of him…"

"No, it'd be the perfect distraction. I kinda want to investigate every nook and cranny of that ship, since it seems to have some significance in whatever transpired with Reginald. But I can't do that unless somebody keeps Dag distracted for me…"

Sally wrung her hands. "I've never really talked to him before. Just watched from afar. It'll be so awkward!"

"The more awkward the better. Come on, it'll be fun."

Sally served Abigail a cup of black coffee, along with a blueberry scone. She nibbled at her own scone as she contemplated it. "Oh, fine. If you insist. You really are Granny's granddaughter. You can get people to agree to anything."

"Hey, who knows, maybe you two will hit it off." Abigail

smirked then tried the scone. It was perfectly sweet and soft, much to her surprise. "Wow. The scones I've had in the past are usually drier than hardtack."

"I make my scones to serve. The freshest you'll ever have."

"I'll say." Abigail indulged herself with the filling treat, periodically taking a sip of coffee that had a complementary hint of berries in its aroma. Soon she was filled up, giving her newfound vigor. "All right, let's do this. My third interview for the day."

"Wow. You should be a PI."

"I sort of am. Well, I'm an insurance claims adjuster, which is like a really boring version of a PI. Shall we head out?"

Sally finished her scone, took in a deep breath, then said, "Yeah. Just promise to save me if I make a total buffoon out of myself."

Abigail didn't have much experience as a wingman—or wingwoman, rather—but she'd do her best. "Just be yourself, Sally, and I'm sure he'll be delighted."

Sally blushed and followed Abigail out, locking the door behind them.

ABIGAIL AND SALLY stopped in front of the ship, staring up at its massive masts. "It looks even bigger up close," Abigail said, and Sally nodded in silent agreement.

No tourists in sight. Just them, the creaking ship, and the

soft splashes of the sea.

That was when Dag popped out of what looked to be the Captain's Quarters. He was a stout man, but muscular, tanned, and bearded, his long hair tied back in a braid. Though he looked gruff on the surface, his baby blue eyes had a young and friendly look to them. "Visitors!" he announced, heading for the gangway.

Sally made a move to turn and run, but Abigail caught her elbow and brought her back in. "Hi," Abigail said, trying to sound perky and unsuspecting. "Is this a bad time for a tour?"

Dag shook his head. "It's as good a time as any. This time of day, this day of the week, you've got the whole ship to yourself."

Perfect. Abigail headed up the wooden gangway, holding onto the rails for dear life as she stole a quick glance at the water below, before finally stepping foot onto the swaying ship. "Wow," she said, the view from the deck really giving her a feel for the size of the Lafayette. "This boat's like straight out of a movie."

Dag shrugged. "She's been in a few. So before I show you around, what's your names?"

Abigail stuck out her hand in greeting. "I'm Abigail, Mrs. Lane's granddaughter." Dag gave her a hearty handshake. "And I assume you know Sally?"

Dag cocked his head, studying Sally's sheepish face. "Only seen her from afar, peering at me from her shop window." He winked at her, and Sally's cheeks grew redder.

Sally said, trying to rescue her own dignity, "I'm just a fan of the ship. Maybe from far away it seems like I'm staring at you, but no, I'm not! That would be totally creepy of me." She laughed forcefully.

Dag snickered and winked. "What was I thinking? Of course you were enamored by the Lafayette. So why don't I give you a more intimate look at her? I'm Dag Madsen, by the way. Brother of Kirby Madsen, who runs the Madsen Candlepin Lanes down the road."

He then led the way down the other side of the deck, where they got a nice view of the sea and the many islands that served as a buffer for the town's coastline. "You see those islands?" he asked, and the two nodded. "Very rocky waters around them. Most captains steer clear of the islands, but this ship had famously dropped anchor near the islands unharmed. This was back before depth gauges made it easier to find safe routes."

Abigail wondered, "What made the Lafayette able to do that?"

"A good captain and a unique ship design. The Lafayette can offload her ballast so she draws less water. Her keel is also retractable."

To Abigail, that sounded like a lot of trouble to get to those islands. She asked, "Anything of interest there?"

"Just beauty. They're mostly untouched by man, given their difficult accessibility. The Lafayette makes trips down there on special occasions, during high tide. Not really open to the public though, since we want to preserve the islands."

Dag turned and motioned they follow him up the steep stairs to the front of the ship. "Come, I'll show you the part everyone wants to see."

Once they cleared the stairs, Abigail saw what he was referring to. A polished and intricately carved wheel protruded out from the middle of the deck, its size and beauty a thing to behold.

Dag gave them a mischievous look. "I usually don't tell the tourists this, but since it's just you two…" He pointed at the center of the wheel, which had a carved scene of a whale and an octopus duking it out. "This isn't just decoration," he suggested, then motioned that they touch it.

Sally caressed the wood carving while Abigail leaned in for a closer look. She noticed some grooves and a sort of gear-like pattern. Sally moved aside, letting Abigail put her hand on the raised part of the carving. Abigail then gave it a twist.

Dag butted in, twisting the carving back. "Well, I didn't mean to actually activate it!"

"Activate what?"

"It's a trap, designed to sink the entire ship."

Abigail gasped and took a step back. "Don't tell me I almost sunk a historical ship!"

"It does take a few more motions than a twist, but yeah, that was a little too close for comfort."

Sally commented, "You should super glue that in place. Doesn't seem like good ship design."

Dag laughed. "Yeah, but then that'd destroy the historical

value of it. See, it's a safety measure. If the ship was ever boarded by pirates, *particularly* Lebeau pirates, the Captain would have the last-ditch option of sinking the whole thing and the treasures it held."

Abigail blinked. "Jeez, talk about going overboard."

Dag laughed a little too hard at her awful pun. "Actually, I think that's where the phrase originated from! Back in the day, the Fischers despised the Lebeaus enough to sink their own ships if it meant keeping their goods out of pirate hands. It was quite the rivalry, for sure."

Abigail decided to make her move now. If a tourist showed up, she wouldn't be able to get Dag talking about his brother, so she had to act fast. "So, Dag. Do ships run in the family?"

Dag looked off in a reverie, long wisps of some loose hair sweeping across his face in the breeze. "Actually, they do. It's the Viking blood in me. There's nothing that feels more right than the wind blowing through my sails."

"You're Kirby's brother, right? Your accent isn't as strong as his."

Dag's facial features softened. "Yeah, he's a bit older than me, by ten years. He was five when our parents moved from our home country to America, so he lived in the homeland just long enough to catch an accent."

Abigail mulled over this new information. "What made your parents move to a whole new country?"

"Father made the move for better opportunities. Though... it wasn't as easy as he thought. The business struggled, until Kirby was about nineteen, when Father handed him the keys to the house and business."

That struck Abigail as odd. "Why would he do that?"

"Greener pastures. Father and Mother took off to mine gold in Alaska. Guess it's that Viking blood in us… Left me here with Kirby when I was only nine. They said they'd be back in a year or two, after they struck gold, but that never really happened."

Abigail shook her head. And here she thought her mother was an irresponsible parent. "I can't believe they would leave you behind at such a young age."

"My parents are pretty odd, I'll admit. But even when they did live with us, Kirby raised me more than anyone, so it wasn't a big change."

Sally put her hands up to her chest. "Still, that must've been so hard for you two, having to become independent at such a young age."

Dag gave a little shrug. "Kirby's got a natural work ethic. Though, I feel kinda bad for him… I get to have a job I love, keeping this ship in top condition. Meanwhile, Kirby feels like it's his duty to keep the family business going. I've offered to help run the place, but he insists I do what I love."

Abigail looked down at the deck, unable to look Dag in the eye after she had suspected his brother of murder. But nobody else came close as a suspect, and perhaps Kirby's love for his brother could drive him to do something terrible… Reginald made accusations about Kirby's donations to the Lafayette, after all.

"He seems like a nice guy," Abigail admitted.

Dag smiled proudly. "He is. Few people see past his rough exterior, but he's an admirable man if you look deeper."

Abigail looked at her watch. "Uh oh. Looks like I gotta cut this short. Grandma will have my head if I'm not home for dinner."

Sally and Dag exchanged quick disappointed glances at each other, and Sally said, "Thanks for the tour."

"Not a problem," Dag said with a charming smile, seeing the two back to the pier.

Once Abigail and Sally made it down the street, Abigail nudged Sally and said, "I think the ice is officially broken."

"Yeah, it wasn't as awkward as I thought it'd be. He's really nice. I was kinda hesitant to meet him because of what a bummer it'd be if he wasn't as charming as he was handsome."

Abigail rolled her eyes. "Invite him to your cafe sometime, you doof. I don't think he'll say no."

"Yeah, maybe," Sally said, fiddling with her keys. "Anyway, you get any useful information out of that?"

"Dunno, I'll have to run it by Grandma, see if she thinks there's a clue in all that. She's sorta my partner in crime."

"Oh, shoot, and here I thought I was!" Sally said with a playful nudge. "Anyway, come to my shop sometime again before you leave town, you got it?"

"Will do." Once Abigail was alone, she sat in her car and stared off. Whoever the killer was, she really hoped Kirby had nothing to do with it.

CHAPTER TWENTY

A bigail returned to the antique shop with her findings. Grandma was in the middle of adjusting a set of porcelain dolls when she let out a little "Oh!" upon seeing Abigail. She moved over to the counter and leaned on it, ready for some new clues. "Tell me what you learned."

Abigail took a seat on a stool at the counter, giving Thor ear rubs as she mulled it over. "Honestly? I don't know. I learned nothing that absolves Kirby, except that he's a hard-working guy who cares deeply for his brother."

"We already knew that."

"Yeah, but it's motive if Reginald was threatening Dag's livelihood in any way. He was snooping around, asking about the ship, which Kirby's apparently donated a lot of money toward preserving. Reginald must've thought the

Lafayette was the key to something, because he was questioning why Kirby was so invested in it."

"Well, I don't know what business a sleazy man like Reginald would have with a historical ship."

Abigail rested her chin in both hands, which caused Thor to whine, glutton for ear scratches that he was. "Beats me. But did you know that ship has a self-destruct mechanism of sorts?"

"Goodness, no. Why would it?"

"On the wheel there's a sorta special carving that if you twist it the right way, like a puzzle box, I guess it opens up a trap that sinks the ship. That way, the ship's cargo stays out of pirate hands, Dag said."

"Very curious. I'm not sure the average cargo haul for a ship like that would be worth sinking it. Perhaps there's more secrets to discover within her hull?"

"Yeah. Not sure how one could go about searching for secrets though. Dag watches over that ship like an overbearing mother."

"He sleeps in the Captain's quarters too. That man's inseparable from that ship!"

Abigail laughed. "Wow. And here I thought Sally stood a chance with him. Sounds like he's already married to the Lafayette."

Grandma walked over to Abigail and squeezed her shoulder. "Well, at least we scratched some suspects off the list today. It's a shame we still aren't sure about Kirby, but we'll hold off until we've got more information."

"I agree."

Grandma flipped over the closed sign. "Time for dinner. I already have a casserole heating up in the oven."

"Sounds delicious." Abigail followed Grandma to the back, past a 'No Customers' sign into the quaint kitchen. Whatever was cooking smelled like potatoes, meat, and cheese—the perfect meal for such a long day.

Abigail took a seat at a small wooden table that had already been set for two. Now seemed as good a time as any to bring up something she had been wondering about for so long. "So Grandma. We haven't had a chance to talk about…" Abigail hesitated. "Well, I don't really know how to ask. But I was wondering what happened in the past, with you and my mom. And Grandpa, I guess. When I first showed up, Sally told me that he'd passed away a while ago."

"Yes," Grandma said, her tone hard to decipher. Abigail picked up a hint of sadness, and a hint of inevitability. Had they not been so happily married?

Grandma donned some oven mittens and pulled out the casserole. "I suppose I can't avoid this topic much longer, can I? And it's not fair to you to be kept in the dark."

"It's not you who's been keeping me in the dark all these years. But Mom has told me next to nothing on the topic. She'd always get fuming mad if I asked about you guys, especially when I was just a girl."

Grandma set the casserole on a cast iron trivet between them before sitting down. "It wasn't one thing, not really. No single explosive event, so to speak. She was a tough kid. 'No,' was her favorite word. Stubborn, obstinate. It served her well in some ways. But it wore on me and as she got older, we fought more and more. And the fights became harsher and harsher."

"I'm sorry to hear that…"

"Your grandfather and I, we lived quite humbly for a long while. This house used to be half this size before I converted it into an antique shop and added a whole new section to the back, which was…" She paused as she tried to recall. "I think a little under thirty years ago. Before I had managed to get this business going, your grandfather and I made a very meager living off his fishing. It was difficult work. Your mother didn't respect that, and thought she deserved more."

"Sounds a lot like her."

"And her father felt the same way, sadly. She wanted more and he wanted to give her more and there was ulti-mately no more to give." Grandma sighed sadly. "I loved her dearly. I *still* love her dearly. And it hurt me to ever punish her, and your grandfather more so. What little reprimanding I did to her, he'd counteract straight after. He didn't seem to understand the concept of hard love. That consequence builds character. How would she ever learn otherwise?"

"She still hasn't learned. Everything is someone else's fault…" Abigail poked at her casserole, feeling bad that she had hardly taken a bite, but then again this conversation wasn't conducive to an appetite. "So what about Grandpa?"

"We separated. When your mother became an adult, she made more and more bad decisions, but with a drinking problem to top it off. I had finally had enough of being her safety net. But your grandfather could never say no to her. Neither of us really wanted to split up. We didn't part on angry terms, if you can believe that. We just ran out of solutions. So he left me the house and the boat while he and your mother moved inland where he worked at a factory to support them both. I guess they needed each other more than either one needed me."

"Grandma, no, don't talk like that!"

Grandma stiffened her lip and laughed. "No. No you're right. I went through a bit of a depression after he left, but that's long past me now."

"It's hard to picture you depressed."

"Happens to the best of us. Anyway, soon after that, I decided I owed it to myself to live the life I wanted. So I sold the boat and turned this place into an antique store."

"And what happened to Grandpa and Mom while they lived together?"

"I'm not fully sure. Your grandfather gave me only the briefest of updates. But before he passed away, she had left to join the Navy of all things."

"And after that? What did Grandpa do?"

Grandma solemnly stared at her plate. "He didn't take good care of himself once Sarah moved out. His health failed him not long after that."

"Wow. That's so sad."

"He was almost sixty. Too young to be dying." Grandma paused, hesitating to ask, "So... How is your mother?"

"I'm not really sure. I hardly see her anymore. We talk on the phone, but that's it. She moves around so much, I stopped being able to keep up. And I guess I had to kind of give up on her too and just focus on my own work and life."

Grandma slumped her head and nodded slightly before asking, "Do you like your work?"

Abigail paused, the topic having been on her mother for so long that she didn't expect to talk about herself. "Oh, uh… I mean, it's better than retail. I get to make my own hours. Own my own car. Rent a decent enough apartment."

"But do you like it?"

Abigail shrugged. "I don't think anyone's really supposed to like work. Not unless they're really lucky."

"You know… I could use an extra hand around the store," Grandma said, her tone light and playful, no pressure intended.

"Man, Grandma. You're gonna have to let me sleep on that."

"Unless, of course, you've got strong roots in that city. But I thought I'd give you the option. From what I've seen of you, you're an outstanding young woman, and I'd be honored to have you help with the store."

Abigail blushed and poked away at her food. She certainly didn't have strong roots in the city. Thor was her closest companion, and he could come with her anywhere she went. She had made more friendly connections here than she ever did in all her years living in the city.

It was a tempting offer, but she knew nothing was that

easy. She had a steady salary in the city. Could she really make a living here?

Grandma stood, bringing the casserole to the fridge. "Just think about it. In the meanwhile, I really ought to turn in for the night. It's been quite the day."

"All right. Good night, Grandma. I'll take care of the dishes."

Grandma patted Abigail's shoulder before heading upstairs, Missy in tow.

AFTER SHE FINISHED CLEANING UP, Abigail turned to Thor. "C'mon, boy. We oughta go to bed too." She turned off the lights and headed up, changing into something more comfy. Once she was in a light shirt and shorts, she sat at the foot of her mother's childhood bed and looked around the room.

Why throw this all away? Her mother grew up in such a nice and cozy home—much nicer than the Navy housing Abigail grew up in. Abigail thought back on how often she and her mother would have to move around, never really having a place to settle into, or a town to get familiar with.

What would it have been like to live in one place, to get to know one's neighbor, one's town?

Grandma's explanation for the falling out between her and Abigail's mother seemed to be missing an actual reason. Sure, Abigail knew her mother would cut people off with only the faintest of excuses, but what made her become that way? How could she treat Grandma like that?

Abigail sighed. Perhaps the discordant parenting styles was enough to make her mother a mess. With Abigail's grandfather advocating a hands-off approach with her mother, while Grandma insisted on teaching discipline, that would certainly result in a child picking sides...

She looked up at her mother's childhood desk, where she had found a stack of diaries earlier. What if the answer could be found in one of her mother's entries?

Abigail sat at the desk and pulled out a diary from the top of the stack. Her mother sure was prolific... Ever since she started the diaries at the age of ten, it seemed she made a new entry every day.

A cursory glance of the first diary revealed little; just that her mother loved catching bugs and studying science. Half the content simply seemed to be things she had learned that day.

Abigail moved on to the next diary. Age eleven now, and little had changed. Abigail moved on again. Age twelve. Now her mother had an ant farm and had joined a science club. Age thirteen... Abigail slowed her reading down, thinking she might have found something relevant.

'So, Diary,' the entry began. 'I met a boy. He's pretty cute, a grade ahead of me. He used to think I was a total nerd, but decided to talk to me today because he likes the band on my T-shirt. I'm playing hard to get, though. Told him I don't

date drummers. If only he knew I haven't dated anyone
before!

'*Could he end up being my first boyfriend? He let me borrow*
a cassette tape that was in his Walkman. He doesn't know, but I
don't have a cassette player. Or much of anything, really. I'm
going to tell him I liked the music though when I see him at
school tomorrow. Ta! P.S. His name is Bobby.'

Er... Bobby was a common name, right? At least that was
what Abigail told herself. But Bobby Kent was the right age,
and it *was* a small town.

Abigail settled in, wondering if this boy was the start of
her mother's tensions with Grandma. She scanned until she
found a particularly smudged page dated six months after
the previous entry she had read.

'*Dear Diary. Bobby found out, and he told me we're done. He*
said he 'doesn't play those games.' What does that even mean? I
thought he'd jump at the opportunity to prove his love to me, but
instead he rejects me?

'*Now I'm stuck with Howard. I don't even like him, I just*
thought it'd spice things up. Bobby hasn't kissed me after all this
time, so I thought he just needed a push. Figures he'd wimp out!'

Abigail sighed and started scanning the content again.
These tactics her mother employed were all too familiar, and
to think little Sarah Lane started so early. The entry went on
for pages, with no mention of either parent.

Her eyelids were growing heavy, and she was no closer to an answer, so she set the diaries aside for the time being. Did her mother really change just like that? From a bright young girl obsessed with insects and science, to a teenager playing mind games with innocent boys?

Abigail liked to think there was a reason behind everything, but perhaps some things just... happened. And if that were the case, it really was a shame.

CHAPTER TWENTY-ONE

A bigail awoke to the sound of Missy giving somebody downstairs a what for. Thor groaned and gave Abigail a look, as if to say, "Let me go down there and set her straight."

"It doesn't matter," Abigail said with a yawn. "I'm awake now. Let's go see if she's barking at someone who deserves it, or if it's just another false alarm."

She rolled off the small bed and tossed on some clothes. Thor took the lead, heading down the steep stairs like a runaway train. Abigail made her way down after him, seeing Sheriff Wilson and Grandma talking in a side room.

Sheriff Wilson turned, the crinkled skin around his baggy eyes making him look like he hadn't slept in days.

"Abigail," Grandma said in greeting. "You've come down just in time. Willy has some news."

"Oh! One moment." Abigail couldn't tell from Grandma's tone if the news was good or bad. Most likely Sheriff Wilson had yet to reveal it, with Missy's rapturous welcome only now coming to a stop. So Abigail let Thor out, then stood next to Grandma, awaiting the news.

Sheriff Wilson fiddled with the frayed rim of his hat. "Okay. The reason I've come here this morning is because I'm plain stumped."

Grandma asked, "How's that?"

"I discovered some things that I think you could further enlighten me on. I really ought to not tell you too many details considering this is an active investigation, but then again, you are an expert on these things..."

"Out with it, Willy," Grandma said, poking him in the side.

"All right, all right. So I found a bunch of letters on Reginald's person. Old ones, one side of an exchange between the Lebeaus and the Fischers."

"Whose side?"

"From a Fischer to a Lebeau, from what I could gather of their context. It wasn't signed. Must've been a secret exchange, considering how cryptic they were."

"And?"

"The letters kept referring to a map hidden within a ship. It was a bit of a riddle, but I mulled it over until something clicked."

"*And?*" Grandma prodded. Abigail could understand her

impatience. Sheriff Wilson had a roundabout way of getting to the point.

"I concluded the map was hidden inside the Lafayette. So I headed over to the ship to see what I could find. Dag was very cooperative and helped me search her high and low. We weren't having much luck, and then it hit me."

He didn't continue, waiting for a reaction. Grandma was at her wit's end. "Oh, out with it already!"

"I realized the map wasn't in the actual ship, but rather in your model of the Lafayette. Conveniently enough for me, I had it stored away in evidence, so I pulled it out, took a gander, and what do you know? I discovered that the model could be opened up. There's enough room in the hull to hide something inside it... A small folded map, for instance."

Grandma exchanged a look with Abigail. "My word. So the broken bottle wasn't an accident after all."

"That's my current theory, anyhow. Another thing, the letters mentioned Dead Man's Cape. That's the old name for those islands off the coast."

Now Abigail had something to contribute. "Dag told me those islands are like nature preserves. A bit too treacherous for your average boat to traverse."

"That's right," Sheriff Wilson said. "And I think the map must've led to some sorta treasure buried somewhere in the Cape. The letters kept mentioning something of value, hidden away. So whoever has that map, they know where the treasure is, and I'm worried they very well could have dug it up already and skipped town."

"But not just anybody can travel those waters."

"I know. It's still in the realm of possibility though. We're keeping an eye on the islands now, just in case. But somebody else knew about the map, and that somebody killed Reginald."

Abigail looked down at her feet, wondering if she should tell Sheriff Wilson what she had learned yesterday. Grandma seemed to know what was going through her mind, and she nodded in solemn encouragement.

Abigail nodded back, before saying, "I really don't want to implicate him, but I know not long before Reginald's murder, he and Kirby got into a heated argument regarding the Lafayette. Exactly what the argument was about, I don't know."

Sheriff Wilson flipped open a notebook and jotted something down. "I see. I'll look into that. I gotta follow any lead I can get, considering how much time has already passed."

He put his hat on then gave the both of them a casual salute. "I'll leave you two to it. Be careful, would you?"

Grandma smiled. "Of course, Willy. You stay safe too."

He headed out, leaving Abigail and Grandma to ponder in silence. Abigail really hoped she didn't just send Sheriff Wilson down the wrong path, but time was of the essence.

CHAPTER TWENTY-TWO

A lone again, Abigail and Grandma shared a quizzical frown. Abigail spoke first. "Some stuff's starting to connect, huh? Whatever this is about, the murder's related to this whole Lebeau and Fischer feud."

Grandma nodded. "Makes me wonder if we're on the wrong track. A Lebeau or Fischer has to be involved... right?"

"It at least starts with a Lebeau or Fischer. The letters and map are key to this whole thing. And you know who's connected to both the map and the letters?"

Grandma didn't need a hint. "Piper. Why don't I call her?"

Abigail hesitated—not because she didn't think Piper could be instrumental in solving the case—but rather because she wanted time alone with Grandma. But then again, this whole thing was rather fun, and would give them some memories they'd never forget…

"Yeah, call her."

Grandma walked over to the hanging rotary phone. She dialed up Piper, smirking at Abigail as the other end connected. "Piper? Oh, I have some awful news, but I don't want to share it over the phone. Would you come over?"

Abigail watched Grandma's face, seeing that Piper's answer was an affirmative one.

"Good, I'll see you soon." She hung up the phone and turned to Abigail.

"Awful news?"

"Oh, that the sheriff will be keeping the model in evidence. The model Ernest had of her family's ship. I'll be so distraught about it that Piper can't help but tell me whatever she must to make me feel better. And *that's* when we strike about the content of those letters!"

Abigail's eyebrow arched in disbelief. This old spitfire sure knew how to work people!

PIPER ARRIVED in a puttering old Ford. She must've pushed that antique car to the limit, because she spared Grandma and Abigail no time to refine their interviewing strategy.

Piper rushed up the steps, her frizzy red hair in a tussle. "What is it, Mrs. Lane?"

Grandma motioned that she follow them into the kitchen, where they could all sit down. Piper took her seat, looking like a wind-up doll whose spring was about to snap.

Grandma put on a somber expression. "That Lafayette model Ernest gave me for safekeeping... Well, it seems I won't be getting it back from Willy, at least not until this murder business is squared away."

"W-why not? Does it have the murderer's fingerprints on it or something?"

"Oh, if only it were that simple. No, it seems to be a key component to some elaborate treasure hunt."

Piper frowned, her pert face somehow becoming more pert. "Um. Treasure hunt?"

"You don't know? It seems there's some important piece of treasure tied into your family's history. Your family, and the Lebeaus."

Piper had no words.

Grandma pressed further, "The model had a map inside. A map to a treasure, no doubt. Sheriff Wilson had surmised as much from the letters he found on Reginald."

"That's weird. I never heard anything about any sort of treasure."

Grandma leaned forward. "And yet Reginald did. I wonder how he knew?"

Piper's lips tightened into a straight line.

"Cookie?" Grandma offered, almost menacingly.

"N-no, thanks, Mrs. Lane."

"Tell me what you know, Piper. Is Reginald some long-lost Fischer?"

Piper shot straight up. "No! I wouldn't be able to live with myself if I were in any way related to that slimy... beady-eyed... miscreant!"

Abigail laughed. "Wow, you really hate that guy."

Piper groaned. "Do I ever. Not that I would murder him or anything."

"Remind me again why you hate him so much?"

"He bought those old letters from Ernest a while back—letters that my great great grandfather wrote. I have the Lebeau side of the correspondence, tucked somewhere safe in the family museum, but they hardly make any sense. If I had the Fischer side of the correspondence, I figured maybe I could piece everything together, but Reginald robbed me of that chance by buying the letters himself and not letting anyone look at them."

Grandma noted, "Those letters are in police custody now."

Piper tilted her head. "Oh? Well, I guess that's better than them being lost."

"Those letters mentioned something rather curious. They spoke of a hidden compartment inside the model. They're the only reason why we know my ship in a bottle used to have a map inside, before Reginald apparently broke it open and stole it."

Grandma and Abigail both watched Piper's face for a reaction. However, instead of any sign of guilt, she seemed to be coming to a realization. "Do you want to hear about a bit of family history that isn't quite common knowledge?"

Grandma did a terrible job of hiding her enthusiasm. "Why, of course, Piper."

"Okay, so you know how it's sorta this thing, how the pirate Lebeaus and the whaler Fischers are the greatest maritime rivals in this coast's history?" Piper sighed. "While that sells a lot of memorabilia and books, it turns out that the two original patriarchs of the family actually didn't hate each other so much. At least, not in their later years. They had come to look back on their rivalry with a sort of fondness."

"Is that so?"

"Yeah. But unfortunately their children still hated each other. Still did whatever they could to sabotage one another's businesses and riches. In the end, it had left the Lebeaus destitute, which only deepened the rivalry. But the two original patriarchs... In the letters I have, it seems they lamented the hatred that they had unintentionally sowed into their families. It had started out as a friendly rivalry, nothing more. The letters mentioned something cryptic about a plan to bring the families together... And I'm thinking... Maybe this treasure was it?"

Grandma frowned. "Interesting."

Abigail wasn't so easily pleased. "Why didn't you tell us all this before, Piper?"

Piper looked like a thief in the spotlight. "I-I didn't know it was relevant. At least, not until Mrs. Lane told me about her ship model having a map in it. I mean, I could have tried cooperating with a Lebeau to see if we could figure out what this plan was, but I thought it'd be too risky."

Abigail thought about it. "Yeah, but how many Lebeaus are left in this world? Isn't Lee pretty amiable?"

"Sure, but I had discovered this information back when Ernest was still alive, and knowing what a self-serving jerk he was, I wasn't about to work with him. Then after he died, leaving Lee as the last Lebeau... I didn't want to dredge up the past after Lee had lost both his parents, you know?"

"And Reginald?"

"Reginald, being the little vulture he was, probably *did* read the letters, looking for anything he could profit from. And that's how he must've learned about Mrs. Lane's ship in a bottle."

Abigail and Grandma shared an impressed look. It all seemed to be coming together—not that they knew what any of it meant. At least, not yet. "So," Abigail prodded further. "Anything else we ought to know, Piper?"

She thought about it. "I only know what the Lebeau side of the letter exchange revealed. I don't know a thing about the map, but as far as the treasure goes... The letters did mention something about a special key. A key in Fischer possession, but where it is, I couldn't begin to guess. It's safe to assume the treasure chest requires a key."

Abigail asked, "Well, anybody who has the map can forgo the key, can't they? I mean, just hire a professional lock picker and presto, right?"

Piper smirked. "That'd be too easy, don't you think? Actually, the letters mentioned something about a fail-safe mechanism if someone tried to force the lock. I'm thinking acid or something that would destroy whatever's inside. So you can't forgo the key to get to the treasure."

Abigail huffed. "Sounds really elaborate. And reminds me of another very extreme fail-safe..."

Piper adjusted her glasses. "What do you mean?"

"I mean the Lafayette has some crazy mechanism on its wheel that can sink the whole boat."

"I... never heard about that."

Abigail nodded. "Might not be common knowledge. Me and Sally got Dag rambling his mouth off, and that's when he mentioned something about the wheel. If you look at it, it's got a really elaborate wooden carving on it, which is actually a puzzle that activates a trap."

"A trap that sinks the whole ship?"

"Yup."

Piper looked like her gears were working overtime. "How odd. I'm going to have to look into that. I suppose these fail-safes ensure both sides of the families cooperated to find the treasure..." She stood from the table. "Would you two mind if I cut this short? This is the most exciting discovery I've had in a while, so I want to head back and comb the family archives for any more information."

Grandma stood and showed Piper out of the kitchen. "You do that—and let us know if you find anything juicy."

Piper laughed. "You're my favorite person to share juicy

information with, Mrs. Lane. Of course you'll be the first to know."

Once they were alone, Grandma turned back to Abigail. "I oughta strangle her, keeping such interesting history from me!"

CHAPTER TWENTY-THREE

A bigail and Grandma continued the rest of the day without much pep. A few customers came and went, but the rumor mill seemed to be taking a break in regards to the murder.

Friday evening was coming to a close, leaving Abigail with only the weekend before she had to return home. She felt no closer to the truth, and worried that the perpetrator had already found the buried treasure and hightailed it out of town.

Abigail had half a mind to call work up and ask for an extension, even if it was unpaid, but she knew that wouldn't turn out well. She was replaceable to the company, and if she pushed it, she'd be among the unemployed.

Grandma came up behind her as Abigail was arranging some antique books. "Dear, is something wrong?"

Abigail turned to face Grandma. "Just wish I could stay longer is all."

Grandma nodded with understanding. "Me too, sweetie. Me too…"

The bell above the front door rang, announcing a customer. They both turned, having to shield their eyes from their visitor's ridiculously radiant smile. The man asked, "Still open, I hope?"

Grandma laughed. "For you, Bobby, there is no closing time."

Abigail took a moment to remember the man's face. Bobby… Bobby Kent, Sally's father. His suit was about the most garish thing she had ever seen, save for the first time she saw him.

"Sorry I haven't stopped by for a while," Bobby said, helping himself to one of the cookies Grandma had out on the front counter. "It's been so hectic down at the news station. All hands on deck, so to speak, even though I'm just the Sunday bingo host."

Abigail asked, "Your newscaster friends having any luck finding leads?"

"Not yet, but they're in a frenzy trying to be the first to break the story. Everybody's calling in, reporting their neighbor as the potential killer. Would lead one to think this town isn't as quaint as it seems!"

Grandma shrugged in defeat. "It would have been nice to have resolved this murder business before the weekend, but I suppose that's too much to ask for. Anyhow, you ate a cookie, so you know what that means."

Bobby lowered his head. "Aw, jeez, Mrs. Lane, I already have so many trinkets at home…"

"There's always room for one more," Grandma suggested with a little wink. Bobby relented and looked about the shop, stopping by a shelf of old tapes and records.

He pulled out a VHS tape, the cardboard sleeve advertising a highlight reel of old 50s game shows. "It's always good to brush up on the classics," he said, bringing it over to the counter for Grandma to ring up. "I do worry I'm getting a bit stale, hosting bingo every week with the same contestants. I wish the station would let me shake things up a bit, but they're so concerned about losing their longtime viewers."

Grandma put the VHS tape in a paper bag and handed it to Bobby. "It would be wiser in the long run to attract some non-geriatric viewers, wouldn't it?"

Bobby snorted. "See, that's what I've been saying. But my producer says kids these days don't watch traditional television, so I don't have many options."

Abigail watched Bobby take his purchase out of the bag to read the back of the VHS box. She wondered again if he was the boy her mother once went out with years ago. With the silence that fell, she decided she might as well ask. "Hey, Bobby. You ever date my mom?"

Bobby nearly dropped the VHS tape as the question made him fumble. "Sarah? Oh, well, uh…"

Grandma's expression grew rather serious. Perhaps she had never read her daughter's diaries.

Bobby fessed up. "Okay, we did, sort of, but I swear we didn't so much as kiss one another's cheeks, Mrs. Lane! We were very young. I think I was fourteen at the time."

Such an unprompted denial coming from anyone else might've been suspicious, but Abigail knew it was true from the diary entries. Not to mention Bobby's blush suggested he was quite the prude.

Abigail explained, "I ask because I looked through my mom's diaries and came across your name. I wasn't sure if it was you or some other Bobby."

"I'm probably the Bobby she wrote of, I admit. It was such a short thing, but I'm sorry I never told you, Mrs. Lane."

Grandma's face was unreadable for a moment, until she finally gave Bobby a dismissive hand wave. "It's no matter. I actually think you would have been a nice boy for her. I just hope she didn't break your heart too hard."

"At first. But it was a learning experience, I guess you could say. Not that I'm a fast learner, since the next girl broke my heart too."

Abigail wondered if she shouldn't pursue the topic. But considering he had volunteered that much information already, she asked, "What happened after that?"

"Oh, a few years after your mother, I ended up with my high school sweetheart. Got married, moved to California, had Sally, hosted my own cable game show… But things changed, my show got canceled, so I came back here and did local TV instead. Wife didn't like the change in lifestyle. Luckily Sally was old enough to make her own choices, and she stuck with me after the divorce."

Abigail winced. "Jeez, that's a tough break, Bobby."

Bobby shrugged. "It wasn't meant to be." Before the topic could continue any further, his phone starting buzzing wildly, making various prize sound effects from classic game shows. He paused to check it, his smile disappearing as his eyes scanned his phone screen. "Oh, boy."

Abigail and Grandma both hovered over him. "What is it?" Abigail asked.

Bobby read it off to them. "My reporter friend just texted me. She says an employee of Kirby's found a gun behind the counter. It matches the same caliber of bullet that killed Reginald. Sheriff Wilson interviewed the rest of the employees and discovered Kirby wasn't working the night of the murder. It was enough information to take Kirby into custody for questioning."

Abigail shot a look Grandma's way. "We were right."

Bobby asked, "You knew?"

"Well, we suspected," Abigail explained. "We just didn't want to believe it. Kirby seemed like a nice guy."

Bobby shrugged, unconvinced. "Strong, quiet types, you know? Something about a man who doesn't engage in small talk really makes me uncomfortable. You shouldn't underestimate what they're capable of."

"I guess."

Bobby tucked his phone away. "I oughta get back to the station. Thanks for the cookie, Mrs. Lane."

Grandma nodded. "And thank you for your patronage."

Bobby shot two playful finger guns at them before he hurried off, leaving them alone again. Grandma turned the 'closed' sign over and locked the front door. "I can't do work after hearing such awful news."

"Yeah, but I mean, at least they solved the case, right?"

"I suppose. That gives us the weekend to relax... But I wonder if it goes deeper?"

Abigail didn't want to go down another rabbit hole, but she indulged Grandma. "What do you mean?"

"What if Dag's involved too? He has access to the ship, after all, and it's somehow connected to this treasure business. Ever since Reginald bought the letters off Ernest Lebeau, he could have let the little family secret out. I mean, who knows how many people he told about the treasure? And since he and Kirby had that fight, the two could have been in on it together. That is, perhaps, until a little back-stabbing occurred?"

Abigail sighed. "I'd rather not entertain that idea. It's already a bummer that Kirby's involved."

Grandma hesitated for a moment, then nodded. "You're right. It's easy to get caught up in the scandal of it all, but I'd rather not implicate anyone else in this nasty business. Let's just try to enjoy the last couple of days of your visit."

Abigail looked down at her hands. "Yeah. Let's."

As exciting as the whole investigation was, looking back,

Abigail almost wished she had spent the time just sitting around, talking to Grandma all day. She had a lifetime of catching up to do, and she doubted she'd get more than a week off every year to do it.

Then again, without the murder, she wouldn't have gotten the call about Grandma being in the hospital. It was just too bad somebody had to die for her and Grandma to finally meet.

CHAPTER TWENTY-FOUR

The news of Kirby's arrest put quite a damper on things. The buzz that had permeated the town since the body's discovery had since tapered off. Now that everything was more quiet and business had slowed, Abigail was starting to think she could get used to this pace. Two or three customers an hour gave her and Grandma time to relax.

Abigail rested her head on her interlaced fingers, her elbows on the sales counter as she watched Grandma take a feather duster to a shelf of collectibles. "So, Grandma," she began. "Tell me about why you got into antiques."

Grandma paused in her dusting and looked over at Abigail, waving the feather duster as she spoke. "I love the tales antiques tell of various times in history. There's something romantic about it."

"In what way?"

"Well, it seems to me that the days of old speak of slower moments, cherished seconds that people seem to take for granted now." She looked off wistfully. "Not to mention the mysteries that revolve around many antiques. They get me wondering where they came from, what purpose they served, the history they witnessed. There's nothing quite like holding something that came from Napoleon's time, or that belonged to a Civil War soldier."

Abigail smiled. "Is that why you named the store 'Whodunit Antiques'?"

Grandma looked at her, a mischievous glint in her eyes. "Yes, that's one reason. Most people like to hear the story behind an antique, and I like to tell them whodunit, so to speak."

"You're pretty cool for a grandma, you know that?" Abigail stood back up and started organizing the day's receipts.

Grandma chuckled, said, "You aren't so bad yourself," then resumed her dusting. Eventually she made her way over to a shelf full of old handmade stuffed animals. She froze, then shot Abigail a look. "I must be getting old. I almost forgot about this."

"About what?"

"A belated birthday gift I had made just for you!"

Abigail frowned curiously. "Really?"

Grandma picked up a floppy old elephant doll made of a

paisley fabric. "I had him made for you when I found out you were born. Sadly I never had the chance to give him to you. You see how his trunk is up?"

Abigail nodded.

"Well, that's for good luck. And it's just for you."

"No kidding? I had noticed him my first morning here, and that he didn't have a price tag. I didn't know you could sew such cute little stuffed animals."

Grandma smiled. "Technically, I *had* him made for you, rather than made him myself. My childhood friend, Mrs. Applebaum, made it." She handed the floppy elephant over to Abigail. "And now it's yours."

Abigail held it tight to her chest. It was ridiculously soft, but also delicate, so she handled it carefully. "Thank you, Grandma. Your friend is very talented."

Grandma nodded. "I miss her so."

"Oh, I'm sorry. I didn't know."

Grandma blinked at her. "Didn't know what?"

"That she had passed...?"

Grandma snickered. "Heavens, no. She's just off on some trip. She's almost always away."

Abigail carefully placed the elephant back on the shelf. "Okay, well, if he's a good luck charm, I think he should stay right here for now."

Grandma smiled, only for them to be interrupted by a customer. They turned, seeing Reginald's business partner enter.

"Are you open?" he asked, despite having already barged in.

Abigail took the lead. "Yes. Can we help you?"

"I just came to ask, hopefully for the last time, what Reginald bought here. Now that his killer has been caught, I thought maybe you two would be more willing to talk."

Abigail crossed her arms and noted, "You don't seem that choked up about it."

He laughed incredulously. "We all grieve differently. Now can one of you help me? I know he spent a lot of money here, almost a thousand dollars, but on what?"

Grandma walked behind the counter and put on a much friendlier demeanor than Abigail. "All sorts of things. Was he your brother?"

The man stuttered for a moment. "Look, I'm about to contact the credit card company to charge back whatever he paid you—that is, *if* I don't get a copy of the receipt."

"You can't do that," Abigail began to say, before Grandma gently squeezed her shoulder.

"It's all right. I'll give the man a receipt, if his card matches Reginald's."

The man nodded, handing his credit card over to Grandma. She bent down behind the counter and pulled out her hand-written sales report. "Gregory Grimes," she mumbled, getting his name off the card as she looked at last week's receipts. "Well, you're certainly related with that name."

"I'm his cousin. Though our relationship was more professional than familial."

"Regardless, I'm sorry for you loss." Grandma's eyes then lit up. "Ah, here it is." She turned the receipt over to Gregory, though she kept a finger on the tip of it, only letting him look.

Gregory looked over the receipt, mumbling, "An old cannon ball?"

"Fired from a Lebeau pirate ship."

"Like the one at the pier?"

"That's a Fischer whaling ship. But similar."

Gregory grumbled, reading further. "A ship wheel? For $500?"

"It's a genuine wheel, again, from a Lebeau pirate ship."

"He wasn't one to spend so much money on a whim. Was there anything special about it?"

Grandma shook her head. "Beside its age and history, though I would think that's enough to make a thing special."

Gregory seemed unconvinced. "Oh well. He must've thought he was on to something, but I don't see how a cannon ball and ship wheel can be worth coming all the way down here for."

"He wanted something else of mine, but I told him it wasn't for sale."

Abigail leaned forward, watching Gregory's expression. She knew Grandma was referring to the ship in a bottle.

"What was it?" Gregory almost demanded.

Grandma left him in anticipation for a few moments

SHELLY WEST

before saying, "Oh, it doesn't matter now. It's in the sheriff's evidence vault. Perhaps you should speak to him?"

Gregory glared at her, then Abigail, then turned around in a huff. "Whatever. As long as the killer has been caught, I suppose I'll try to put this whole mess behind me." With that, he stormed out.

Abigail watched as he peeled away in his car. Once he disappeared, she turned back to Grandma. "Think we should tell the sheriff about him?"

"I don't think he'd have volunteered his name had he been involved in any of this."

"Still, he seems a little odd."

"Well, people can be odd when they're grieving, like he said. We have his license plate, phone number, and name. If we catch a whiff of anything else that might be suspicious, we'll hand the information over to the sheriff, but otherwise, we should leave him be. He lost a cousin and a business partner."

Abigail shrugged. "I suppose…"

"How about we wrap it up for the day?" Grandma asked. "We can walk the dogs for a bit and take in the afternoon air. The poor things must have cabin fever."

Abigail noticed Thor jump up when he heard Grandma say the word 'walk.' Missy, on the other hand, huddled into the corner.

Abigail laughed. "You did it now, Grandma. Thor just heard the 'w' word. Missy doesn't seem as excited, though."

170

"She's never liked the thought of exercise, though once she gets out there, she ends up enjoying herself."

"Yeah, I think a walk will be nice for all of us." Abigail grabbed two leashes hanging from an antique hall tree, then called the dogs over to get them ready. Grandma pulled on her cozy red cardigan while Abigail put on her raincoat, then they led their leashed dogs out of the store.

OUTSIDE, Abigail locked arms with Grandma as they carefully walked down the steps, the sidewalk, and then turned right. The dogs pulled them from one nice smelling object or bush to another.

"Whoa there, pups," Abigail said while trying to catch her breath. "Let's pace ourselves."

Thor turned his head back at her then huffed, as if exasperated by their slow pace.

They walked a few blocks, Grandma regaling Abigail with information about the owners of stores and homes as they passed by. Eventually Abigail noticed Grandma's voice becoming more tired as they ventured farther, so she decided to turn around to head back home.

Missy and Thor caught on to the change in direction and together slowed their pace. Grandma observed, "I believe we have us two cohorts in crime."

"And what crime is that?"

"Lollygagging when we have a warm fire to return to." Grandma winked.

"I believe you're right. I wonder if the 't' word might quicken the little criminals?"

"That just might do the trick," Grandma replied. She stopped walking and addressed Abigail with a loud uptone. "Do you think Missy and Thor would like some *treats*?"

Abigail played along. "Hm. Jeez, I don't know, Grandma. I think they'd rather stay outside."

Missy tried getting their attention, spinning and dancing on her hind legs, begging for them to look down.

Thor, who wasn't known for being an excitable dog, did the most excited thing he could think of and sneezed. Not once. Not twice. But three times!

"Okay, okay!" Grandma relented. "A treat it is!" She gave Abigail a sideways glance. "I think they'll hurry things along now."

An hour later, Thor and Missy were fast asleep by the fireplace. Grandma and Abigail wrapped up a dinner of New England clam chowder and freshly baked yeast rolls, served with a warmed cider.

After they cleaned up the dishes, they sat by the fire, reading from their books for a short while before Grandma yawned and suggested it was time to turn in.

Abigail felt already so at home with Grandma. She dreaded the morning when she would have to return to Boston.

"Time's going by too fast," Abigail later said as she lay in bed, looking toward the curtained window. Her gaze followed the light from the moon which shined on Thor, who slept peacefully at the foot of the bed.

She whispered to the sleeping giant, "This feels like home, doesn't it, boy? I'd hate to leave."

Eventually she managed to fall asleep.

CHAPTER TWENTY-FIVE

The next morning, Abigail awoke to the familiar groaning of an old man. "What in the world?" she mumbled as she sat up, realizing that this perceived old man was actually Thor barking his head off at the window.

"Jeez, Thor, why can't you bark like a normal dog? What's with the groaning and moaning?"

Thor paid her no heed, his moaning worsening.

"Only been around Miss Yipsalot for a week and you already picked up her bad behavior, huh? Nothing's worth getting this hysterical about."

Thor stopped for a moment, eyeing Abigail as if he took issue with being compared to Missy, before giving a low ruff.

Abigail got out of bed and looked out the second story window, scanning the quiet road for whatever had Thor so upset. "You seeing things, boy?"

He nudged her aside, his eyes honing in on his target.

"Oh." Now Abigail saw it. A cat. "That's it? You usually don't bark at just anything. You're about to lose your window privileges, mister."

Thor insisted, continuing to point with his eyes at the cat.

Abigail looked more closely and gasped. "Oh! The poor thing's missing a leg!"

She hurriedly put on some clothes, tucked her phone into her pocket, then quietly padded off down the hall, trying to not wake up Grandma. Could the cat have been hit by a car? Attacked by some coyotes? Gotten a little too friendly with a lawnmower? She almost didn't want to imagine what could've happened.

Abigail shoved her feet into Grandma's slippers and headed out the door, slowing her approach to not scare the lumbering cat.

But the black and white cat didn't seem the least bit frazzled. In fact, as it limped around Grandma's roses, it looked like it didn't have a care in the world.

"Oh," Abigail said, seeing that whatever had happened to its leg, it must've happened a long time ago. The three legged cat looked anything but injured.

She kneeled and put her hand out, expecting the cat to be skittish. Instead, it let out a comically deep 'mrrrreow' and moseyed on over to her, rubbing against her legs.

"You're an odd-looking fella," Abigail remarked, petting him, then noticing he had a collar. She lifted him up and read his tag to learn his name. "Blackbeard, huh?"

He meowed in confirmation. Abigail could see how the name fit him, what with his missing leg and black muzzle.

And boy, was he hefty. "You look a bit too pampered to be an outside cat."

She noticed a neighbor sitting on their porch, and figured she ought to ask, "Hey, any idea whose cat this is?"

The neighbor squinted. "Oh yeah, that's Lee's cat. He lives down the road, in that nautical-looking house." She pointed. "I rarely see Blackbeard outside, though."

"Is that so? Guess I'll return him." Abigail shifted the heavy cat in her arms and walked off, her mind abuzz. She had no clue that Lee lived so close, or that he was a cat person. That might've explained his distaste for Thor.

"Now, what could your owner be up to that he forgot about his kitty, hm?"

Blackbeard had no response. For a moment Abigail worried she wouldn't be able to tell his house from one of the many neighbors, but then she saw it: A house that looked like a freakin' boat.

"Well, that's ridiculous."

Blackbeard started squirming in her arms as she approached the house, so she let him go and followed him up the sidewalk. That was when she noticed the front door was wide open.

"Huh." She watched Blackbeard scurry inside and wondered if she should follow him.

Something was definitely not right. The whole thing

reminded her of the night when Sheriff Wilson found Missy outside with Grandma's door wide open.

Abigail cleared her throat and stopped in front of the doorway. "Lee?" She waited, but received no answer. "Lee?" she said again, this time loud enough to ensure he couldn't sleep through it.

She wasn't sure if she should step in. It would be trespassing, wouldn't it? But then again, what if he was in trouble?

Abigail wrung her hands, not sure what to do. The last time something like this happened, it produced a dead body. Though she didn't have a good first impression of Lee, she really didn't want him to end up with the same fate. She had to make sure he was okay.

So Abigail stepped in, announcing her presence loud and clear. "I'm coming in, Lee. Don't shoot me, okay? It's just me, Abigail. You remember, the only person in this town who takes her coffee black."

She reached the back of the house, having seen no evidence of a break-in or struggle. "Well, this is just plain weird."

Abigail took out her phone and headed for the front door. She did her due diligence, but now it was time to involve the authorities. With a killer on the loose, one couldn't be too careful.

She dialed the sheriff.

"Sheriff Wilson," he answered rather hurriedly.

"H-hi. It's Abigail."

"Are you okay?" he asked.

"Yeah, I'm fine, I just—"

"I know we thought we had the killer in custody, but I was wrong. So I hope you're somewhere safe."

"What?" Abigail glanced around, feeling like the killer could be right behind her. "Are you serious? What about Kirby?"

"The markings on the bullet didn't match the barrel of his pistol. Well, err, I really shouldn't be telling you that, but I just want you to know you need to be careful."

"You let Kirby go, then?"

"Yes. We're back to square one."

Abigail felt an odd sense of relief, considering. "I'm glad he didn't do it. Oh! But I'm calling you because Lee's missing. His door is wide open, just like Grandma's was."

"Where are you?"

"At his house. I was returning his cat, and—"

"Get back to the antique store. I'll come investigate in the meanwhile. You and Mrs. Lane need to watch out for each other."

"O-okay."

Sheriff Wilson hung up.

Abigail hesitated, then decided to close the door so that Blackbeard didn't get out again before she hurried back to the store.

~

ABIGAIL CREPT into Grandma's room, finding both the elderly woman and Missy snoring in unison. She wondered if she should wake them, but decided against it. There wasn't much either of them could do now anyway.

She headed back downstairs with Thor, letting the dog out for his morning business. She sat out on the porch stairs, one cheek resting on her hand as she scrolled on her phone. And here she thought she'd get to enjoy the weekend without any more of this murder drama.

Her phone buzzed, the caller ID revealing it to be Sally. "This early in the morning?" Abigail mumbled to herself before answering. "Hello."

"Abi!" Sally said, her voice all choked up.

"What is it?"

"Dag's gone!"

Abigail frowned, straightening up. "How do you know that? Maybe he's just sleeping in."

"I know he's missing, because the Lafayette's missing too!"

Abigail jumped right up. "How does a big boat like that go missing?" she almost shouted, now matching Sally's tone.

"I don't know!"

"Okay, I'm coming down. Gimme a second."

She ended the call then whistled for Thor. He galloped over, awaiting her command. "You watch the house, you got it, boy?"

He let out a low ruff.

Abigail grabbed her keys before remembering Grandma. She took a moment to run up the stairs, this time not hesitating to wake the woman up. She opened the bedroom door, saying, "Grandma! You won't believe it."

Missy whimpered as Grandma groaned herself awake. She rubbed her eyes and grumbled, "Oh, did you *have* to wake me up? I was dreaming about Humphrey Bogart and things were just starting to get steamy!"

Abigail lost all train of thought for a moment. "Uh. Kirby's innocent. The Lafayette is missing. And so is Lee. And Dag. I can't sit around here—I have to see what's happening."

Grandma's eyes grew wide. "Oh! You must! I'll hold down the fort. You go get 'em!" She quickly added, "And Abigail?"

"Yes?"

"Be careful."

Having received Grandma's blessing, Abigail shot her a thumbs up and tore down the stairs.

CHAPTER TWENTY-SIX

A bigail arrived downtown within a couple of minutes. She found Sally and Bobby outside the Book Cafe, sitting at one of the outside tables with... Dag? Abigail parked and got out, a quizzical look on her face.

Sally waved her over, explaining, "Abigail! I thought Dag was missing, but my father found him out by the pier."

Abigail looked Dag over, seeing the normally confident and handsome man doubled over in grief. She asked, "Okay, so what happened?"

Dag mumbled, "I got my brother back, but now I've lost the Lafayette. It seems like I'm cursed, doesn't it?"

"Now, let's not get superstitious here. Did you report the missing ship?"

Bobby was already on the case. "I called it in straight

away, but Sheriff Wilson's investigating a house that was broken into."

Lee's house. "Oh. But he's coming, right?"

Dag nodded. "Yeah, said he's gonna round up the Coast Guard, but it's pointless. The ship's long gone."

"When did it get stolen? Don't you sleep inside the Captain's Quarters?"

"Yeah, I do. Whoever took her knocked me out, tied me up, and left me on the pier. I only managed to break free of the ropes half an hour ago, then Bobby saw me a little after that."

"Who attacked you?"

"I don't know. It was dark."

"Why would someone steal her?"

"Beats me. I mean, besides her being the most beautiful ship at sea, she only has historical value. It's not like her thieves could sell her off or whatever, not without being caught. She isn't like a stolen work of art; you can't sell her underground. She's huge."

Abigail stared off at the shore, seeing how bare it looked without the Lafayette. "You don't just steal a ship like that for no reason."

"Tell that to whoever took her."

Abigail's absent stare turned into a pointed glare. "She's the key."

"Key? Key to what?"

"A long-buried treasure. It's a long story, but it's got to do with the old Lebeau and Fischer rivalry."

Dag and Sally looked at each other, neither of them following Abigail.

Abigail turned and put both hands on the table. "Look. That wheel's gotta be the key to the treasure chest. That's why removing it would sink the ship, because you're supposed to bring the ship to the treasure. Both Fischer and Lebeau are supposed to cooperate."

Dag blinked hard, trying to comprehend her. "What treasure are you talking about?"

"Oh, that's right. You guys don't know, but Grandma unknowingly had a map to a buried treasure chest—a map that was stolen. And according to Piper, the ship somehow has the key… or is the key, to the treasure chest. The chest is rigged to destroy everything inside if you don't use the key. The original heads of the Fischer and Lebeau families came up with this treasure hunt as a way to get the two families to cooperate."

Dag shook his head. "Sounds far-fetched. If the ship wheel contains the key, one could have just put it in dry dock and remove the wheel without the risk of it sinking."

"But nobody would know to do that, unless both the Lebeaus and the Fischers cooperated and shared what they knew. The Lebeaus had the treasure map, while the Fischers had the key. At least, they did before the ship became historical town property. But either way, neither family would get anywhere without cooperating. Unless, I suppose, somebody stole the map *and* the ship…"

"Which is where we are now," Dag concluded.

185

Sally asked, "Then where's the treasure?"

Abigail looked toward the foggy horizon. "Somewhere off in those islands."

"Dead Man's Cape?" Dag asked. "I suppose that's as good a place for buried treasure as anywhere else."

Bobby was hanging onto every word the three of them were exchanging. He finally interjected, "We must sail to those islands, before it's too late!"

Everyone's expression grew serious, until Sally said, "Dad, there's no way."

Bobby stood up. "Of course there is. My boat, The Little Kahuna. It's only big enough for two people, but it's a sailboat. It can navigate Dead Man's Cape with ease!"

Dag stared off at the ocean, the distant islands obscured by fog. "It is possible…"

Sally was already on the phone. "Don't you guys do anything crazy, okay? I'm telling the Coast Guard to look there."

Dag stated, "The Coast Guard doesn't know those islands like I do. It's very rocky waters, dangerous to navigate quickly, unless you know the exact path to take. Which I do."

Bobby grabbed Dag by the shoulders and shook him. "Then take her! I bought The Little Kahuna a while back, fancying myself a fisherman. But after catching nothing but seaweed, I left her languishing there for years! She deserves some adventure."

Dag looked down, a man defeated. "I hardly deserve to

sail a fishing boat, much less the Lafayette. I can't believe I let her get taken on my watch…"

It was Abigail's turn to shake Dag by the shoulders. "Dag, you're the best sailboat captain in town, aren't you? You've got that Viking blood in you. Come on, where's that salty dog spirit? We need to go before whoever stole the ship snags the treasure and hightails it out of town!"

That got Dag moving. "A-all right! I'll go, but someone needs to come with me to help with the sails."

Abigail didn't hesitate a moment. "I'll go." She turned to Bobby. "Where's your boat?"

He pointed toward the pier. "The Little Kahuna is the blue and white one. Hurry!"

Dag and Abigail gave each other one last look, then took off for the pier.

"But be careful!" Sally called after them, a little less excited about this adventure than her dad.

Abigail almost laughed. Careful? Today, she didn't know the meaning of the word.

CHAPTER TWENTY-SEVEN

D ag captained The Little Kahuna with grace and ease, swinging the sail just the right way to catch the wind, cutting through the fog on their way to Dead Man's Cape.

Abigail held onto both sides of the rather small vessel, wondering if her high school swimming lessons would be enough for these choppy waves. "What's the plan if we see the Lafayette?" she asked, thinking that *maybe* she should have pondered this before getting on the boat.

"The Lafayette has a secret entry point on her side. We can sneak in through there."

"And if she's sunk? I mean, they could have gotten what they needed and activated the trap."

Dag paused breathlessly. "Let's not consider that, all right?" He then lowered the sail, stating, "We're getting close, if she is in the cape. Be ready. We're going to be outnumbered."

"What?"

"It's a three-man operation, at the very least, sailing the Lafayette. And three skilled men at that."

"Maybe we should've considered that before coming this far."

"I count for two men, wouldn't you say?"

Abigail considered it, concluding, "At least you have high self-esteem."

"That, and I know the Lafayette better than anyone. We have the advantage. Still, be careful."

"So three people, huh? I don't even have three suspects in mind."

"Whoever they are, they must be skilled sailors. That's all I know."

"Would you consider Lee skilled?"

Dag shrugged. "Average."

"What about... Antonio?"

"Who?"

Abigail looked toward the sea, starting to get a hunch. "The guy who works for Lee. Fixing boats and yachts."

"I don't know him. Maybe."

"He *is* new in town. That alone is something to suspect."

Dag glanced over his shoulder at her. "Okay, but that's only two men. It's impossible to get this far without three. The Lafayette is a big lass, too big for two sailors to wrangle."

Abigail grew suddenly quiet. So quiet, that Dag forgot to steer the ship for a moment and scraped a rock.

"What is it? The look on your face nearly made me crash!"

Abigail finally found her words. "I know who the third man is. Come on, we gotta hurry! If I'm right, Lee's on that ship against his will, and they'll probably throw him overboard once they get what they need!"

DAG MADE HASTE, and soon they cleared the foggy waters to find an unsettling sight: the Lafayette run aground among some rocks.

Dag let out an involuntary whimper, unfitting of a man his size. "That's no way to treat her."

Abigail knew they didn't have time to lament. "At least she's on ground and not about to sink. Come on, we gotta get closer."

Dag steered The Little Kahuna around, coming up behind the Lafayette in complete silence. He pointed at a lighter colored section of wood. "That's the secret entrance."

They both held their breath when a sudden shouting erupted above on the Lafayette's deck. Dag turned to Abigail and whispered, "Follow me. We'll get the jump on them."

Abigail opened her mouth to protest, but Dag didn't waste a second more. He dropped anchor, opened the secret entrance, and jumped in. Abigail muffled a groan and followed, not about to be left behind.

Inside the ship, it was pitch black. Abigail grabbed Dag's arm despite herself. "I'm about to have a heart attack."

"Just follow me," Dag whispered, navigating the dark interior with ease.

He stopped at a ladder and waited, listening. Once he pinpointed their location above deck, he hurried up, stopping to crack open the trapdoor and get a peek at the action.

Abigail watched from the bottom of the ladder, her heart pounding.

"Three men," Dag whispered, confirming their suspicions. "They're all facing away. This is our chance."

He carefully opened the trap door and pulled himself up. Abigail followed, the only thing giving her any courage being that this guy was a modern-day Viking, and that this ship was the love of his life.

Once she pulled herself topside, she nearly gasped at what she saw. The three thieves all had their backs turned, facing a comically huge treasure chest. She felt oddly vindicated to have been right about who the three were, but that didn't make it any easier to accept.

The first two men were Lee and Antonio.

The other man was somebody Abigail had never seen before, but still, she knew who he was.

Even from behind, she could tell the stranger was related to Lee. He was an older man with a grim disposition, who Lee kept shrinking from.

The man was Lee's supposedly dead father, Ernest.

And when she noticed the gun in Antonio's hand, she knew for certain that Lee didn't want to take any part in this. He had been forced to help them sail here, kidnapped from his own home, by his own father.

Ernest was impatiently trying to fit an oddly shaped key into the treasure box. Antonio shifted from one foot to the other, not looking too keen on sticking around here for long. "Let me try it."

"Shut up!" Ernest snapped, resuming his sad attempt at shoving the key in.

Dag whispered to Abigail, "I'm grabbing the man with the gun. You stay behind cover in case things go south."

Before Abigail could argue, Dag took off, taking careful steps as if he knew exactly which planks creaked.

Not a soul heard his approach.

When he snatched the pistol from behind Antonio, all three men just about jumped out of their boots.

"Haha!" Dag said with aplomb as the three of them gaped. "How nice of you to find the treasure for me. It'll bring in a staggering amount of tourists, which *might* make up for the fact that you ran this old girl aground."

"Idiot," Antonio said, staring at the gun. "You don't want to get involved in this mess. It runs deeper than you or this old boat."

Dag snarled. "She's not a boat. She's a ship!"

Sirens gave them all pause, and as the fog started to clear, they saw the Coast Guard making a slow and careful approach.

Abigail decided to reveal herself, making Ernest and Antonio jump yet again. Lee gasped at the sight of her. "Abigail?"

"That's right, Lee. I've got your back." She then narrowed her eyes at Ernest and couldn't help but chide him. "You should be ashamed."

The man glared at her. "What?"

"You led your own son to believe you were dead, and why? Just to throw everyone off your tracks as you hunted this treasure down?"

"And just who are you?"

"I'm Lee's friend."

Lee's face softened upon hearing that. "Really? Your friend?"

Abigail shot him a look. "Yeah, but don't push it." She then turned her attention back to her suspects. "You and Antonio went through a lot of trouble, and took advantage of your own son, all for what?"

"You're wrong." Ernest turned his gaze to Lee. "My son's the one who held us at gunpoint. Isn't that right, Antonio?"

Antonio nodded, but Abigail simply scoffed. "Nobody's going to fall for that. Lee never even had the letters."

"What letters?"

"The letters Reginald got from you. The ones found on his body." Abigail crossed the deck to Lee's side.

Ernest scoffed. "I don't know what you're talking about."

"Come on. Those letters were hardly a secret. You flaunted them to Piper, then sold them to an antique dealer she hated."

"They were mine to do with as I wished. And what do the letters have to do with this?"

"The letters hinted at a map. You didn't know it, but Reginald figured it out and in his excitement, he told a few people. Word of the map must've eventually gotten to you, which enticed you out of hiding."

Ernest rolled his eyes. "That'd make me quite the mastermind, wouldn't it?"

"It's not a stretch. You've been after that map for years. Piper told me you hounded her for any hints about it. So when the man you sold the letters to for a quick buck uncovered the answer, you decided to take your chances. You come from a pirate bloodline, after all. It's made you quite the opportunist."

Ernest's chest swelled. Abigail wondered if it was swelling with pride, or with anxiety.

She continued, "Then, I assume, things went awry and Reginald ended up dead."

She watched him closely. Ernest's eyes shifted to Antonio, who suddenly grew rigid.

"I didn't do it," Ernest mumbled under his breath, his eyes still on Antonio.

Antonio's face showed a mix of shock and anger. "You would sell me out? Seriously? This was all your plan. I didn't even want to move to this no-name town!"

Ernest snapped, "Shut up, you moron. I'll get us both a good lawyer, but you need to shut up!"

Abigail's fists clenched. "Wow, a lawyer? You really are a coward. First you lie to your son about your death, then you're happy to let Kirby, an innocent man, take the blame for Reginald's murder?"

"I'm not saying anything else. Let the authorities handle this, girl. All your evidence is circumstantial at best."

Dag's demeanor was as disgusted as Abigail's. "Yeah, until they do forensics on this gun and match it to the bullet that killed Reginald."

Ernest stiffened, but before he could respond, a couple of Coast Guard officers managed to row their way up to the Lafayette and started boarding. "Guess your grand adventure's over," Abigail said, letting herself enjoy Ernest's downfall. "Not many adventures to be had in jail, buddy."

Ernest laughed and put his hands in the air as the officers surrounded him. "We'll see."

Sheriff Wilson managed to climb up the ladder to the ship. He had on an inflatable life vest, and looked anything but comfortable as he tried to keep his balance in the light sway of the water. "I told you to stay with Mrs. Lane," he said pointedly to Abigail.

"She told me to go get 'em."

Sheriff Wilson sighed. "Of course she did."

One of the Coast Guard officers confiscated the key from Ernest, turning it over as he cocked his head. "What's this?"

"A key," Abigail answered. "Sheriff, do you mind if I open the treasure box?"

Sheriff Wilson nodded. "Of course. Let's see what this whole circus was about."

The Coast Guard officer handed her the key, then Abigail walked over to the treasure box, kneeled, and fit the wooden piece inside the lock. Dag walked over to her side, helping her lift the heavy lid, and they both stared in awe at the ancient relics inside.

Sheriff Wilson gave an impressed whistle from behind Abigail. "I'm no historian, but that stuff looks mighty old."

Dag hazarded, "That cat statue looks Egyptian; the coins look Roman or Greek. And that dagger... an ancient medieval weapon, perhaps?" He shrugged. "I was expecting gold, but these must still be pretty valuable."

"All right," Sheriff Wilson began. "Let's start clearing this ship out." He then nodded at the rest of the officers to take the thieves into custody.

Abigail noticed they were cuffing Lee. "Wait a minute. He had nothing to do with any of this. They had him at gunpoint when we first sneaked on board."

"Is that right?" Sheriff Wilson looked over at Dag for confirmation, then nodded, ordering to one of his men, "All right, uncuff him. Lee, I still need a statement though."

Lee nodded and said, "Okay, Sheriff." He looked rather glum, watching in silence as the officers took his father away.

Sheriff Wilson waited until Ernest and Antonio were

secure on the Coast Guard boat, then he ordered, "Take Abigail, Dag, and Lee separately. I don't want them interacting with each other until I get their statements."

Abigail cooperated as a couple of Coast Guard officers guided her to a rowboat. It wasn't quite the hero's treatment she thought she'd get for solving the case, but then again, she understood why Sheriff Wilson was being cautious. She was merely a citizen, after all, an out-of-towner who got caught up in probably the biggest heist this town had ever seen.

CHAPTER TWENTY-EIGHT

That afternoon, Abigail sat on the rocking chair, rocking in rhythm to the ticking clocks as she idly pet Thor. Grandma stood at the checkout counter and sighed, having tried everything to calm Abigail's nerves.

"How about I bake you a fresh batch of cookies? Think that'll make you feel better, dear?"

Abigail looked up. "I'm fine. I'm just processing everything is all. I mean, I just re-commandeered a whaling ship with the help of a Viking. I'm not sure I'll ever be able to top that. I've peaked."

Grandma chuckled. "You'd be surprised what kind of excitement this town experiences daily. So no cookies, then?"

Abigail politely shook her head. "I don't like sweets that

much. I mean, they're fine in moderation, just not for every meal."

Grandma looked like she was about to have a heart attack. She mumbled to herself, "Was she switched at birth, perhaps? There's no other explanation."

Abigail began, "I *do* know a couple of people who could use some cookies though."

Grandma straightened up. "Oh?"

"Kirby and Lee. Lee's probably still busy dealing with the fallout of everything that happened, but I can at least pay Kirby a visit and apologize."

A sparkle returned to Grandma's eyes. "Just give me fifteen minutes, and I'll have a fresh batch ready to go!"

She hurried off to the kitchen, leaving Abigail to wonder how one could make homemade cookies that quickly. Abigail looked over at Thor, and they both shared a silent moment before she said, "I can't stand the mystery any longer. I gotta know what's in her secret recipe."

Thor wagged his tail in agreement.

"I'm gonna take a peek. You stay here."

Abigail tiptoed toward the kitchen, avoiding the spots of the floor she knew creaked. She held her breath and peered around the doorway, seeing Grandma rummaging around in the fridge. That made enough sense. Cookies required eggs to make, and the eggs were in the fridge.

But then Grandma pulled out something unspeakable: a *tub* of *premade* cookie dough!

Abigail couldn't help herself. She gasped, "Grandma!"

Grandma spun around, the tub in her arms as she squeaked, "A-Abigail!" She shot a glance at an open window before hurling the tub through it with the precision of a professional quarterback.

What followed was silence as Grandma stared tight-lipped at Abigail. Eventually Abigail managed to ask, "What was that?"

"What was what?"

"The thing you just threw out the—"

"You saw nothing!" Grandma said with a stamp of her foot. "Now, if you wouldn't mind, I need to head outside for some fresh air."

Abigail moved aside as Grandma headed out for some 'fresh air' that just so happened to be in the general area as the thrown tub. Once Abigail was alone, she told Thor, "This might be the scandal of the century, boy. Grandma's famous cookies… are store-bought!"

Thor let out a horrific howl, as if to say, "Hush! Such secrets could get a fellow killed!"

'FRESH' cookies in hand, Abigail stood in front of the Madsen Candlepin Lanes. She took in a deep breath and entered.

She found Kirby by himself, leaning over the counter, watching the news on a wall-mounted TV. He glanced at her curiously.

"Hi," Abigail managed to say. She lifted the tray of cookies, which piqued Kirby's interest.

"Well, this is unexpected. The lady of the hour."

"I feel like I owe you an apology." She set the tray down next to him.

"Why would that be?" Kirby asked, his accent still a bit intimidating, as innocent as he might have been.

"I think I'm the one who might've sent Sheriff Wilson your way."

Kirby frowned.

"I had heard about your confrontation with Reginald, and thought maybe that was relevant to his murder."

Kirby's frown deepened and deepened... then he burst out laughing. "Me, murder him? Why would I need to murder someone when I can simply stare them down?"

Abigail nodded. Kirby's stare was indeed terrifying. "I heard he made threats about the Lafayette, asking why you had donated so much to its preservation. Though now I understand why; you're just supporting your brother."

Kirby nodded. "Yes, but I'm thinking I won't need to support him much longer. Look." He turned the volume up on the TV.

Abigail watched. On screen was footage of the Lafayette and Dag, along with the treasure chest.

Dag demonstrated to the reporter how to open the intricate treasure chest using the oddly shaped key found on the wheel. Inside was plunder from ancient tombs of various origin. The reporter identified each piece of treasure,

202

starting with a small Egyptian figure of a cat, a Viking dagger, and a pile of ancient Roman coins.

The footage cut to Bobby Kent, with the words 'Bobby's Big Bingo Host' below him. "That's right, it was my Little Kahuna that saved the Lafayette! It may not be tourist season, but there's no better time to come on down to Wallace Point and see a real life treasure chest!" He aimed two finger guns at the camera and flashed a brilliant smile, holding the pose until the footage finally cut.

Kirby muted the TV and turned to Abigail. "Thanks to you, I have a feeling business is about to pick up. And who knows, maybe with this new treasure chest attraction, the Lafayette will have enough visitors that she won't need my donations anymore."

Abigail gasped. "I didn't think of that. I guess there's an upside to this whole thing then."

Kirby smiled. "One night in custody wasn't such a bad price to pay. And I get a tray of Mrs. Lane's famous cookies to top it all off."

Abigail forced a smile. "Yup!" She worried what might happen if Grandma's cookie secret ever got out. "Well, I ought to go. Nice seeing you!" she said, hurrying to leave before she spilled any beans.

Kirby waved her off with a smile, none the wiser.

CHAPTER TWENTY-NINE

S unday morning arrived all too fast. Abigail looked around her mother's childhood room, wondering when she'd get to visit this town again. She forced herself out of bed and reluctantly put on the final outfit she had packed. Had it really been a week since she first got here? She could hardly believe it.

Abigail paused as she passed her mother's desk, and decided to take one last look at the diaries. She skipped a few years' worth of notebooks, going straight to the final one. She had to do the math on her mother's age compared to the date on the first entry, concluding her mother must've been sixteen.

The entry was full of unfamiliar names, some girls, mostly boys.

'I'm sick of this town,' it read. *'I bet everyone's less boring in the cities. Stacy's life has gotten more exciting since she moved. Her letters go on and on about Broadway, cruises, bands she gets to see live. Meanwhile I'm wallowing away in a one stoplight town.'*

Abigail stopped reading and moved on to the next entry. It was dated a year later.

'Mike's got a place in Providence. I'm moving in with him the second I get my GED. Yup, I'm graduating early. Why waste another year of my life here, right? You've seen what it's done to me. I don't want to end up like Mom and Dad, working endlessly, not doing anything exciting.'

Abigail saw that the rest of the pages were blank. Her mother must've left soon after.

"What a little—" Abigail stopped herself. "I'm calling her up," she told Thor, then dialed her mother. She didn't know exactly what she was going to say, but she had to say something.

She waited for the inevitable redirect to voicemail.

But this time, her mother actually answered. "Abigail?"

"Yeah, hey Mom. You're up early."

"I switched shifts with Jessie. Are you back?"

"No, I'm still with Grandma, though I have to leave today."

Her mother didn't respond immediately. "Oh. Well. I

hope she hasn't told you too many tales. Wallace Point is a drag, isn't it?"

"If sneaking aboard a historical ship and solving a murder is a drag, then jeez, I guess so."

"What?"

"Grandma's doing fine, by the way," Abigail stated, her tone carefully measured.

"Good. I'm glad you two are getting along."

Abigail somehow doubted that. "You should talk to Grandma. There's no good reason for cutting her off."

Her mother sighed loud enough to distort the sound coming out of the speaker. "Yeah, well, I have to go. I need to catch the bus."

"She misses you, Mom."

Her mother said nothing for a long moment, before saying, "All right, I really am running late."

Abigail decided not to push it. "Okay. Talk to you later."

"Bye, hun."

Her mother hung up. Abigail wondered why her mom never gave an inch. Was she really that rotten, or was she just ashamed? Embarrassed? Her mother had, after all, informed Abigail about Grandma's accident. That had to show she cared, if only a little, right?

Abigail decided she had dwelled enough on her mother. As much as she liked to think there was a direct cause to everything, she worried that some people were simply no good. Ernest, Antonio, her mom… She just hoped her mother never ended up like the other two, and instead would patch things up before it was too late.

"C'mon, Thor," Abigail said, heading for the downstairs kitchen.

ABIGAIL SAT at the table in the kitchen, moping over a bowl of cereal as Thor snaked his oafish self around the table and chair legs.

"You don't wanna go, huh, boy?"

Thor sighed.

"Yeah, me neither."

Abigail's cereal was getting soggy, but she didn't have the appetite to eat it.

That was when Grandma came in, holding a newspaper. "Oh, good morning. You're up."

"Yeah. Procrastinating packing my things."

Grandma smiled softly and sat across from Abigail. "When do you think you'll have another week of vacation time saved up?"

Abigail shrugged. "Sometime later next year."

"Maybe you could take a week unpaid, and I'll cover the costs?"

Abigail forced a smile. "That's nice of you, Grandma. But if I take too much time off, the company might start seeing me as dispensable."

Grandma squeezed the newspaper, crinkling it. "I just

can't stand the way hard workers are treated these days. If you worked for me—"

"I doubt that'd be smart for your bottom line. I mean, adding on an extra employee isn't going to net you enough sales to be worth it."

"Oh, I hate that kind of talk. I just want to see you more. And if you're really concerned about my bottom line, well, just this one week of you being here has brought in more customers than I normally see in a year!"

Abigail paused. "Really?"

"You'd be doing me a favor."

She looked away. Now she was running out of reasons to say no. "You know what, Grandma? I'll think about it. It's a big decision, but I'll really think about it. As long as you're sure you won't get sick of me and my moaning dog."

Grandma chuckled. "I'd be the happiest old coot in town." She unfolded the newspaper, looking over the front page. "Oh, looks like Lee has been cleared of all suspicion. Antonio fessed up to the murder, with Ernest being charged as an accomplice. I guess it's safe to leave the doors unlocked again."

Abigail almost dropped her spoon. "What's with you people? Keep your doors locked, murderer on the loose or not!"

"Oh, that's just the city girl in you talking. There's nothing to worry about."

Abigail groaned at Grandma's lack of concern. Then, as if

to prove her point, the bell above the door rang to alert them of somebody's entrance.

Grandma frowned and stood. "Oh, a customer? This early?"

Abigail followed her out to the front, seeing Gregory, the late Reginald's cousin. His features were softer now, not the suspicious on-guard demeanor he had all the other times Abigail had seen him.

Gregory cleared his throat. "I hope I'm not intruding?"

Abigail gave Grandma a sideways glance. "Not at all. The door was unlocked, which means anyone's welcomed."

Gregory laughed and looked away sheepishly. "I just came here to say thanks. Thanks for figuring out what happened to my cousin. When I had heard that the cops thought he got killed over some petty dispute, it didn't sit right with me. So I'm glad you looked deeper and discovered the real reason."

Abigail let herself take in the praise. "What can I say? It seemed like too easy of an answer. And if I had accepted it— well, a couple of pirates might've gotten away with murder."

"I know my cousin could be a bit... unpleasant to deal with, but he had an insatiable curiosity. Always wanted to uncover some grand mystery, some deadly secret. Just before he disappeared a few weeks ago, he had told me he was onto something big. And, as we see now, he was right."

Grandma commented, "Shame he had to die to uncover this secret, regardless of how pushy and persistent he was."

"He crossed the line when he broke into your store to

grab the ship in a bottle. Not that I think anyone deserves to die for a mistake like that, but at the same time, I get the feeling he knew the risks, and pursued it regardless." Gregory let out a sigh. "Anyhow, if you ever find yourselves in New Jersey..." He handed Abigail a business card, this time without any information scratched out. "That's our antique store. Well, *my* antique store now."

Abigail smiled at him. "Thank you. I wish things didn't have to happen the way they did for us to meet though."

"It's all right. Time to move forward."

He was about to turn when Grandma put a hand on his shoulder. "Wait," she said, before turning to a display where the bottleless ship sat. She picked it up gingerly, before offering it to Gregory. "The Sheriff released this from evidence. I want you to have it, in honor of your cousin."

Gregory blinked and stuttered. "I, uh... Are you sure?"

"Just promise not to sell it, okay?"

"Of course," Gregory said, handling the ship model with care. "Thank you. It means a lot."

Gregory bid his farewell and headed out, seeming to be holding back some tears. Grandma shook her head as she watched him drive off, saying, "I wish Reginald could have learned his lesson without dying."

"He did sorta cross a line, though."

"Regardless."

Abigail changed the subject. "I want to pay Lee a visit. See how he's doing. He must be pretty frazzled, learning that his father had been alive all this time."

"Yes, I'm sure it'd boost his spirit to see you. Let me make another batch of cookies for him."

Abigail laughed and finished up her cereal. "Yeah, I'll leave you to it to make your famous homemade cookies."

"Yes, you'd better."

Abigail grabbed the newspaper for her own perusing and headed out of the kitchen.

CHAPTER THIRTY

Once Abigail had a fresh batch of cookies to deliver, she walked down the street to Lee's house. To her surprise, she found him outside tending to his garden, looking more carefree than ever before. And here she thought the guy would be devastated!

Lee's cat was out with him, and Blackbeard meowed lazily in greeting. Lee turned around, his gloved hands full of dirt, and he smiled. "Hey there, you swashbuckler."

Abigail lifted the tray of cookies. "I thought I'd find you in low spirits, so I brought these cookies." She paused. "But it seems like you're doing okay."

"Yeah. I'll still take the cookies though."

Abigail laughed and set them down on a porch table.

Lee nodded at his cat. "Meet Blackbeard."

"I already did. I found him out roaming the streets yesterday, after your apparent kidnapping."

"Oh. Well, uh, thanks for bringing him back home."

"What happened to his leg?"

Lee shrugged. "Found him that way, when he was just a kitten. He had taken up residence in a boat I was repairing, and when I discovered him, I just had to bring him back home."

Abigail sat on the steps next to him. "So what about your father? That must be quite the shock, huh?"

Lee ripped out a weed. "Not really, when I think back on things. He had a lot of debts, a lot of enemies... Dying was a good way to absolve himself of all that. I just wish he had cued me in on his new identity. He must've known I couldn't keep a secret like that, though."

"What did he plan on doing with you after he got the treasure?"

"I kinda wonder that myself."

"And Antonio?"

"A distant relative, apparently, one just as slimy as my dad. The two of them had been planning this for years. Can you believe that?"

"That's crazy. So how'd you guys find the treasure chest? Did X really mark the spot?"

"Yeah, the map had a few landmarks drawn on it, so my father figured it out from there. They left me on the ship as they went on the island to dig it up. Guess they knew I was stranded and couldn't escape if I wanted to. When they brought the chest on board, I couldn't believe what I was seeing. It really was a full-blown treasure chest. Lucky for me, they had a lot of trouble figuring out how to open it using the key on the ship wheel."

"At least it's all over now. What about the 'good lawyer' Ernest said he'd get?"

"I don't know, but the lawyer's going to have his hands full, because Sheriff Wilson told me the gun does in fact match up to the bullet found in Reginald. I don't think Ernest or Antonio are going to see the outside of a jail cell for a while." Lee paused and sighed. "Sometimes I wish I had a normal, boring family history."

"Yeah, I know the feeling."

"Well, if you end up kidnapped by pirates or something similar, I'll have your back. I owe you one."

Abigail laughed. "I hope it never comes to that. So what's going on with the boat repair shop, now that you're down an employee?"

Lee's answer was swift and sure: "I'm selling it. Before yesterday, I felt like I had an obligation to keep the business in the family—you know, in memory of my *late* father. But now, after I sell the place, I'm going to do what I want to do."

"Which is?"

Lee smirked at her. "I always wanted to be a lighthouse keeper. The local one needs a caretaker, and you know what? It has a garden. Or, well, it used to, back in the day. When I was a kid, that garden was one of my favorite places to visit.

It's all dead now, but I like a challenge, so I'm going to see about restoring the property."

"That sounds awesome."

"And what about you? You going to stay here?"

Abigail stumbled over her words. "I-I—well, you know."

"What?"

"I have a job back in the city."

"Oh."

She looked away, taking a moment to sort her thoughts. "But you know what, Lee? I've been thinking…"

"Oh?"

"I'm gonna take that job—*and shove it!*"

Lee got up to his feet. "Yeah! Life's too short to do what you hate. Take it from me; I got kidnapped by literal pirates!" He held his hand up in the air for her to high-five.

Abigail smacked his hand so hard, she about knocked the twig of a man over. "I have a feeling you're gonna be seeing a lot more of me, Lee. Whether you like it or not!"

"I like it!" Lee said, rubbing his hand.

Abigail turned, eyeing the antique store out in the distance. "I'm gonna go tell Grandma. You enjoy those cookies, skinny boy."

"O-okay, I will," Lee responded as Abigail hurried off.

ABIGAIL RETURNED to the antique shop, in a much different mood than when she had left it. She noticed an antique Ford in the side parking lot, so she wasn't surprised to find Piper talking to Grandma inside.

The two were talking breathlessly, rambling on about the ship, the treasure, and the drama between the Fischers and the Lebeaus.

Piper turned to see Abigail. "You! I'm going to want to record your side of the story sometime, for historical accuracy. This ship heist has been the most exciting thing to happen in our town's history since that one time Lebeau pirates hoisted a cow up into the church bell tower."

Abigail quirked her head. "What?"

"They did it to distract the entire town while a few Lebeau pirates stole from the unattended stores. It was quite the scandal, though not as big a story as this!"

"And here I thought this was a sleepy little town."

Piper shook her head. "This will be quite the attraction. I'm going to donate everything related to the Lafayette's history from my family's collection to the ship's museum. I'd rather share our history with the world rather than keep it to myself anyhow."

Abigail commented, "That's awesome," then noticed Grandma looking at her strangely. She asked, "What?"

"Speaking of interesting stories," Grandma segued. "Piper was just telling me something interesting before you walked in."

Abigail frowned. "And what's that, Grandma?"

"Apparently my shop has recently started instituting a banning policy."

Abigail got shifty-eyed, unsure how that got out. "Oh, that. Yeah, well, Lee had it coming. I unbanned him, though."

"It's not such a bad idea," Grandma mused. "Perhaps if I had banned Reginald, he'd still be kicking."

"So what, did Lee snitch?" Abigail asked, ready to ban him again.

Grandma laughed. "No, he didn't rat you out. He confided in Piper here, and she thought it was so funny, she had to tell me."

Abigail turned toward Piper. "Did she now?"

Piper laughed and slowly backed away toward the store's entrance. "Uh, on that note, I'll see you two later. Bye, Grandma. Uh, Abigail." She waved and left the store, as if fearful of her own potential banning.

Grandma and Abigail burst out laughing. Abigail asked, "I hope you aren't mad at me."

"Actually, I quite like the idea of banning certain folk. It sounds like fun!" Grandma clapped her hands together in merriment before asking, "So, how is Lee doing?"

"Great, actually. It's like he's free now. He's selling the boat repair shop and plans on taking care of an old lighthouse in town."

Grandma cocked her head. "The abandoned one?"

"I guess so."

She smiled softly and looked off. "I'm happy for him."

"He's not the only one making drastic changes in his life…"

Grandma frowned. "Who else is?"

Abigail laughed and wrapped an arm over Grandma's shoulders. "I think I'm done with the city, Grandma."

Grandma gasped so suddenly, she nearly choked. "Y-you mean...?"

"I want to take you up on your offer, if it still stands."

Grandma stood up and gave Abigail a bear hug, almost lifting her off her feet. "Of course it still stands!"

"Easy, Grandma, you're gonna sprain something!"

Grandma stepped back. "It's such a big move though. Are you sure?"

"This past week has been more exciting than my entire life. I'm not about to miss out on what happens next in this town. That—and I want to make up for all the lost time we could've had together."

Grandma sniffled and wiped her eyes. "I'm so happy to hear that, dear." She looked down at Missy, who was guarding her doggy bed, yipping at Thor every time he passed by. "You're going to have to make nice with Thor, Missy. You two are about to become roommates."

Missy groaned as Thor licked her face, messing up her perfectly coiffed hair.

CHAPTER THIRTY-ONE

The move took Abigail less than a week to sort out. She had left Thor with Grandma, not wanting to subject the poor dog to the cramped confines of her car again. She also wanted him to keep an eye on Grandma... just in case.

By the following Thursday morning, she had her VW Beetle packed to the brim. She didn't need to bring any furniture, as her mother's childhood room was fully furnished, so all she had to bring were her clothes, books, and a few other things.

Abigail went through her mental checklist again:

- *Sort out the lease with the landlord—Check.*
- *Search the apartment for anything she might have missed—Check.*

- *Turn in her notice at work and subsequently get fired on the spot—Err, check.*
- *Pay off any unpaid bills—Check.*
- *Return some library books—Check.*

Jeez, being lawfully good was hard work. Her mother would have just upped and left.

But enough about her mother.

Abigail walked through the apartment one last time. Though she had lived in the cramped dwelling for only a few years, she couldn't help but feel nostalgic. She patted the radiator next to her window. "Goodbye radiator that makes *way* too much noise for a radiator."

She paused in front of her fridge. "Goodbye fridge that inexplicably leaks water all over the floor."

She moved on to the kitchen sink. "Goodbye faucet that occasionally spurts out brown stuff."

On second thought, maybe she wouldn't miss this place after all.

ABIGAIL MADE the final drive back down to Wallace Point, arriving in the afternoon. When she parked at the Victorian house and got out, Thor came galloping over to welcome her back. "Hey, buddy," Abigail said, flopping his ears around. Even Missy stood at the front door, wagging her tail in greeting.

But where was Grandma?

Abigail made her way up the porch, her pace quickening until she practically burst through the door.

There she found Grandma poring over a newspaper.

Grandma jumped, putting a hand to her chest as if to hold back a heart attack. "Oh, Abigail! I thought you were someone else for a moment." She got out from around the counter and gave Abigail a huge hug.

"Who else could it be?" Abigail asked with a laugh.

Grandma grabbed the newspaper and handed it over to her. "Oh, just another killer on the loose, apparently."

Abigail frowned and looked at the headline.

The Wallace Point Ripper Stabs Again!

Abigail calmly set the newspaper down, at a loss for words.

Grandma shrugged. "And here we thought he was gone for good. It's one of Wallace Point's longest running cold cases... Though I suppose it's not so cold anymore, is it?"

Abigail sat down on the rocking chair. "I'm just surprised nobody suspects me. Seems these murders only happen when I'm around!"

Grandma smirked, a glint in her eye. "Every great sleuth needs a greater adversary. And with us on the case, this fellow doesn't stand a chance!"

Abigail thought about it for a moment, stood, and nodded with determination. "You know what, Grandma? You're right. Whatever stabby psycho this town throws at us, we're gonna get him behind bars in as little time as it takes you to bake a batch of cookies!"

Grandma pumped her fist. "That's the spirit, dear! Just watch yourself in regards to my cookies. You told me you saw nothing, after all."

Abigail laughed, said, "Sure, Grandma," then headed out to start unpacking her things.

She had a feeling there'd never be a dull moment in Wallace Point.

Don't close the book just yet!
Here's a preview of *A Stab in the Dark* the second book in the *Whodunit Antiques* series, **now available on Amazon.**

Abigail struggled to breathe in enough air while she chased after Thor, her Great Dane. He wasn't poorly leash-trained by any means, but the difficulty of keeping up with him came down to simple math: One of his strides amounted to five of Abigail's.

"Thor," she gasped. "Thor, wait up!"

The Great Dane heard her sputtering call, immediately made an abrupt U-Turn in the middle of the empty sidewalk, and came bounding back toward her. His long legs covered the considerable distance between them in just a few seconds.

Abigail wheezed as Thor licked her hand encouragingly. She had decided she'd never miss a morning walk after moving down to Wallace Point and seeing how nice and quiet it was. Now she doubted her decision.

Thor, of course, was a huge proponent of the walks. Living in a cramped city apartment for years could do that to a dog.

Abigail's lungs burned despite the good breeze, and she felt a serious cramp starting in her side. "That's it," she huffed, slowing from her tortured jog to a more comfortable walk. "No more."

Thor bowed his head, then slowly looked up at her in disappointment.

"Oh, don't take that tone of face with me," Abigail warned, wagging a finger in front of his large nose. "We weren't all built for galloping like you."

Thor sneezed at the compliment, as if to say, "I suppose I won't hold it against you."

Abigail knew the neighborhood better now than she had a few weeks ago and soon they were walking up to Grandma's antique store, Whodunit Antiques. The store wouldn't open for a couple of hours, but the sheriff's car was already parked in the customer lot.

"Look, Thor," Abigail said. "Sheriff Wilson caught Grandma bright and early today, didn't he?"

Thor trotted to the driver's door and sniffed it. He looked back at Abigail, shot her a reassuring grin, jerked his leash from her hands and leaped onto the front porch, where he collapsed into a big, satisfied heap. Abigail shook her head as she walked up the steps, unclipping his leash before she headed in.

The front door was unlocked, as usual. Grandma refused

to lock her doors, even after the store had been broken into during one of the most exciting murder cases Wallace Point had seen in years.

The case started with someone breaking into Grandma's store in search of an antique. Grandma, alerted by her Shih Tzu Missy's whimpering, had come down the stairs in the middle of the night to find the source of the noise. She got more than she had bargained for when she tripped over a dead body.

The fall had landed Grandma in the hospital, which was the only reason Abigail discovered she had another living family member besides her mother, Sarah. Abigail sighed. Her mom wasn't exactly forthcoming when it came to her past.

Sheriff Wilson and Grandma sat at the kitchen table with cups of steaming coffee in front of them and a heaping plate of cookies between them.

"Good morning, Grandma, Sheriff Wilson," Abigail said. She walked to the sink and poured herself a glass of water. Missy greeted Abigail with a quick trot around her ankles and then settled again underneath Grandma's feet.

As soon as Abigail took her first sip of water, she knew that something wasn't right. The room was too quiet, as if Grandma and the Sheriff had stopped talking just before she entered.

"Good morning, dear," Grandma finally said, her eyes still on the sheriff. "How was your run?"

"Awful. But at least Thor enjoyed it." Abigail washed out

her glass and placed it on the drying rack. "Shame on you, Sheriff Wilson, for pulling my sweet Grandma out of bed so early."

Sheriff Wilson glanced up at her. His eyes looked puffy and tired, and it took him a moment to understand she had spoken to him. "Eh? What was that, Abigail?"

Yup, something was definitely up. Grandma usually had Sheriff Wilson's full attention. In fact, Grandma usually had the full attention of most older men. Today, however, Sheriff Wilson was obviously preoccupied.

"Sweetheart," Grandma cut in, "I feel like pancakes this morning. Why don't you take a shower while I whip some up?"

Abigail paused. What was Grandma up to? Was she just trying to get Abigail out of the room? But Abigail only nodded. "Pancakes sound great, Grandma. Just give me thirty minutes."

Abigail didn't actually need thirty minutes, but she wanted to give Sheriff Wilson plenty of time with Grandma.

When she walked back into the kitchen, the sheriff was gone and in his place at the table was a plate full of steaming pancakes. Bits of chocolate formed smiley faces on each pancake. Some faces had freckles.

"So, what's going on with the sheriff?"

Grandma flipped a final pancake onto her plate and eased

into a chair. "He's got skeletons falling out of his closets."

"What?"

"Just the past refusing to stay in the past. You know that stabbing at the motel?"

"The one that happened right when I moved in? Yeah, how could I forget?"

"Well, the newspaper had suggested it could be an infamous serial killer."

"Suggested is an understatement." Abigail finished smothering her pancakes with butter and real maple syrup. "I can still remember that headline. *Wallace Point Ripper Stabs Again!* For a small town newspaper, they do love their gore."

"Yes. It was rather sensational of them. Anyway, Willy has the Ripper on his mind."

"But I thought it wasn't really the Ripper. Something to do with out-of-towners, right?"

Grandma nodded. "The more details that came out, the less likely it seemed to be our local serial stabber. But it still has brought up some bad memories for Willy. He has a complicated history with the Ripper, you see."

"I didn't know that."

"He doesn't talk about it much. It was a tough time for him. You might not believe it now, but Willy was a talented detective. He was on his way up. Nothing could stump him." Grandma looked off, possibly remembering a younger, brighter Willy Wilson. "But then the Wallace Point Ripper came along, and Willy couldn't solve the case. He followed every lead, pursued every angle. Nothing. Since then, he hasn't been the same. He lost his confidence, his spark. I guess you could say it broke him."

"Wow. That's awful."

"It is. Ever since, he hasn't been comfortable with any case that isn't open and shut. And now the big fuss at the motel has brought it all back for him." Grandma refilled her cup of coffee and, without meeting Abigail's gaze, added, "I wouldn't bring it up around him, dear, if you can avoid it."

That was a surprise.

It made sense that Willy wouldn't want to discuss the Ripper. But it seemed odd that Grandma felt the need to warn Abigail away from future conversations. In a town where rumors spread like wildfire, and where everyone else already knew all the details, why the extra caution? Abigail took another bite of her pancakes. "Sure, Grandma. The story is safe with me."

It was a quiet morning for the store—too quiet for Grandma's taste.

"Something's up," she said from her seat behind the checkout counter, her eyes peering sharply into the vacant parking lot. "I'm going to fix a plate of cookies and take them… take them… Well, I'll take them somewhere and find out exactly what's going on."

"You always do, Grandma," Abigail said, pausing from her work researching a colorful Tiffany lamp Grandma had recently acquired at an auction. "We can take my car if you like."

"No, thank you, dear. I wouldn't want to trouble you. Willy probably just lost his cat up a tree again. Last time that happened, he shut down the entire town. And during tourist season too."

"That must be some cat."

"It's twenty-five years old. Going for a world record, I think. Anyhow, I'm going to close for lunch and meet up with the gals."

"Gals?"

Grandma smirked. "You've met them before. I heard that you apparently call them the 'Granny Gang.'"

"Oh, *those* gals. Yeah, well, I had quite the first encounter with them."

"When was this?"

"When you were in the hospital. They arrived at the store in a bunch of golf carts and swarmed the place. It felt like a police raid!"

"How silly. They're just a bunch of old harmless coots. We like to exchange gossip while we sew us up some sock monkeys. Nothing more."

"Sock monkeys? I thought recently you told me you couldn't sew."

Grandma's expression grew dire. "That's right. I can't. My sock monkeys tend to be... How do I put it kindly? Sock monstrosities. I usually end up having to burn them in fear they might come to life and take revenge on their creator."

"Now I kinda want to see one of these things."

"Trust me; you don't. And anyhow, I'm not there for the sock monkeys. I'm there for the gossip."

"Then gossip away, Grandma, and let me know what you find out. In the meanwhile, I think I'll pay Sally a visit."

"Sounds like a plan… And sounds like we'll be pretty busy today. Is Friday Movie Night still on?"

Abigail smiled. "You know I'd never miss it."

Grandma reached out to Abigail for a hug, which Abigail returned. "Just think, two months ago I had never met my granddaughter. Now I get to see her every day."

The walk to the Book Cafe, Sally's coffee shop and rare books store, was short and pleasant. Summer was giving way to autumn, with the first whispers of cool weather kissing the air.

Abigail stepped into the cafe, the tiny bell above the door announcing her entrance. The little shop smelled of fresh coffee and the innermost pages of old books. Sunlight poured in through the large glass windows, tinting everything gold and brown.

Sally stood at the counter, facing away as she spoke excitedly into her phone. Not that there were many customers at the moment. In fact, Abigail was the only one.

Sally Kent made the best coffee Abigail had ever tasted, and so the Book Cafe was rarely vacant, even during the quiet season. Yet here Abigail was, the only customer. Maybe Grandma was right that something was up today.

Abigail, not wanting to interrupt, sought out the book she had been reading from the bookshelf. The Book Cafe acted like an unofficial library of antique books. The books had to stay at the cafe, but customers could read as many as they wanted.

Abigail found her current book, one on steamships from the early 1900s. A blue sloth bookmarker marked her place, and she began reading about the SS Atlantic. This ship was quite a bit larger than the schooner she had saved from pirates during her first visit to Wallace Point.

Abigail paused to shake her head incredulously. Sometimes even *she* didn't believe she had managed to do that.

Sally hung up the phone and whipped around, her blonde ponytail flying out over her shoulders. Her face, usually bright and perky, positively glowed with the excitement of fresh gossip. "Oh, Abigail! Have you heard?"

Abigail closed the book and put it away, suspecting she wasn't going to get any more reading done. "No. What's the buzz?"

"James Wilson is back in town!"

"Who?"

"Sheriff Wilson's son! He just arrived, and after all these years, he's here to help his father with the big case."

"The investigation into the stabbing? I thought that was over."

Sally shrugged, a happy bounce to her shoulders. "I guess not! Now, you know what this means, don't you?"

"No. What does it mean?"

"Fresh meat! You're off the hook as the newbie in town."

Abigail frowned, taking in this new information. The Sheriff's son… If he had been gone all this time, why would he come back now? It wasn't like this stabbing was that big of a case, especially compared to what happened with the ship earlier.

A distant honking pervaded the store, shaking Abigail out of her thoughts. The symphony of horns grew closer and louder, until finally a fleet of old ladies in tricked out golf carts came into view through the big store windows.

Sally whispered in awe, "The Granny Gang. There's thousands of them!"

Abigail stood, getting a closer look. "I would say about a couple of dozen at best."

"Still, you never see them all together like this unless something big is going down."

Abigail squinted, trying to make out the golf cart taking the lead. "Grandma?" she said in realization, but the horde of golf carts peeled away before she could think to go out and greet them.

Sally commented, "Dang, they're on a mission, huh?"

Abigail shook her head in disbelief. "Whatever she's up to, Grandma better not get into too much trouble!"

Grab the full book on Amazon!

ABOUT THE AUTHOR

Mysteries run in the family, starting all the way back to my great grandmother. I grew up watching old black and white movies like The Thin Man and Rebecca, and reading classic mysteries by Poe, Doyle, and Christie.

Outside of writing mysteries, I love old steamships, 1990s adventure puzzle games, and trusty pets. I live in a coastal New England town with my hideous (yet charming) Chihuahua, Fugly.

Made in the USA
Coppell, TX
29 May 2020

26620119R00141